WHO AR

"Hi! Mort Kaufmann's the name. Have you two just wandered into the castle?"

The one with the gun slowly straightened.

"What sort of creature are you?" he barked. "And what are you doing in stronghold of Proconsul?"

"The what of who?" Kaufmann laughed. "You got it wrong. I should be asking what you're doing here—but of course I know perfectly well what you're doing. You were just minding your own business when all of a sudden a wall in your—" He took a step forward and peeked into the opening. "—living room? Yeah, a wall in your living room suddenly went *poof* and a doorway pops out of nowhere. And you go through, and you wind up here, and you're wondering what it's all about. Right?"

The creature thrust the pistol toward him. "I ask you question! Speak, or I will drill hole in your hairy head."

Kaufmann backed off. "Hey, now look. I don't want any trouble with you guys. Just being friendly, is all. I'm just trying to help out. You know, you really shouldn't—"

The unarmed creature rushed him . . .

Castle for Rent

CASTLE FOR RENT

John DeChancie

ACE BOOKS, NEW YORK

This book is an Ace original edition,
and has never been previously published.

CASTLE FOR RENT

An Ace Book/published by arrangement with
the author

PRINTING HISTORY
Ace edition/April 1989

ISBN: 0-441-09406-6

Ace Books are published by The Berkley Publishing Group,
200 Madison Avenue, New York, New York 10016.
The name "ACE" and the "A" logo are trademarks
belonging to Charter Communications, Inc.

PRINTED IN THE UNITED STATES OF AMERICA

10 9 8 7 6 5 4

To Thomas F. Monteleone

The splendor falls on castle walls
   And snowy summits old in story:
The long light shakes across the lakes,
   And the wild cataract leaps in glory.
Blow, bugle, blow, set the wild echoes flying,
Blow, bugle; answer, echoes, dying, dying, dying.

—Tennyson

CASTLE FOR RENT

PROLOGUE

CELLAR, NEAR THE DONJON

IN A NICHE in a crypt deep within a great castle, a section of wall vanished and revealed a high-raftered, pelt-hung room which evoked the interior of a Viking hall—but not quite. Two creatures stood in the room, facing each other. They were not human, but approximated human form. Their faces were huge and wrinkled, their eyes narrow slits over a blunt snout split by a mouth not unlike a hippopotamus', save that the teeth were numerous and sharp. They had thick, squat bodies, exorbitantly muscled, with leathery blue skin. They wore pieces of shiny green armor that could have been plastic or fiberglass or some composite material—or perhaps sections of the carapace of a giant insect. Both creatures wore swords and daggers in ornate scabbards. The behavior and mannerisms of both creatures could generally be described as an exaggeration, perhaps even a parody, of behavior patterns peculiar to a certain type of overaggressive male human.

The sudden materialization of the opening had interrupted a conversation—rather, a confrontation involving bared teeth, threatening postures, and much angry grunting and gesticulating. The creature who faced the opening stopped in mid-gesture, his six-fingered hand raised to strike the other creature. A puzzled expression formed on his inhuman countenance. The other creature had backed off, hand darting to the curving grip of a pistol in a hip holster.

Slowly the first creature lowered his arm, then grunted and motioned toward the opening, which lay at his adversary's back. The other grunted threateningly in reply, warily maintaining his orientation and taking another step back. He wasn't taking any chances. The first grunted again, pointing emphatically toward the suddenly created doorway.

The second creature couldn't resist casting a glance to the rear. He did an almost comic double take and whirled about to face the opening. Their argument temporarily forgotten, the two approached the anomaly. The second creature drew his weapon—a strange thing with a short barrel and a large underhanging clip. Cautiously they peered out. There was nothing immediately outside the opening but the bare stone walls of a corridor running to darkness at either hand. The gun-bearing creature stuck his head out and looked one way then the other. He snorted.

Then he said: "Secret passage. Escape tunnel."

The other grunted something in reply.

The first holstered his weapon and stepped out into the corridor. "Runs directly to Proconsul's quarters, leads to outside."

"Convenient," said the first creature as it came through the doorway. "But where did wall go?" He examined the dark stone of corridor, still looking puzzled. "Wonder where stone comes from. Strange stuff." He thumped a blue fist against it.

The gun-toting creature sniffed the air, snout wriggling. "Something not right here."

The other glanced about warily. "Strange. Very strange."

They wandered about, sniffing high and low, probing cracks and crannies with fat, blunt fingers.

"Sorcerer's work," the unarmed creature pronounced, peering at multicolored glittering motes that lay deep within the stone.

"You think?"

"What else? I saw wall disappear."

"You are drunk."

"If I want excrement from you, I will squeeze it out of your head!"

"And I will make you eat it—along with your words, dungbreath!"

The two squared off and snarled at each other for a spell. Gradually the tension lessened as they were again distracted by the strange apparition.

"Sorcerer's work, I tell you."

"Nonsense. Escape tunnel, nothing more."

"Look at seam here, between stone and wood. Blurry." The creature put his hand up against the juncture and observed that the hand became indistinct, then withdrew it as from something hot.

"Look!"

Far down the corridor, a mote of light danced in the darkness. Soon footsteps approached.

The two creatures went into defensive stances.

"Hi, there!" came a voice from down the hall.

A human approached, a short bearded man in jeans and a T-shirt. He stopped a short distance away. He held an odd lantern: it was a long wooden handle with a huge glowing jewel affixed to the end. The jewel glowed an eerie blue-white.

"Hi! Mort Kaufmann's the name. Have you two just wandered into the castle?"

The one with the gun slowly straightened.

"What sort of creature are you?" he barked. "And what are you doing in stronghold of Proconsul?"

"The what of who?" Kaufmann laughed. "You got it wrong. I should be asking what you're doing here—but of course I know perfectly well what you're doing. You were just minding your own business when all of a sudden a wall in your—" He took a step forward and peeked into the opening. "—living room? Yeah, a wall in your living room suddenly went *poof* and a doorway pops out of nowhere. And you go through, and you wind up here, and you're wondering what it's all about. Right?"

The creature thrust the pistol toward him. "I ask you question! Speak, or I will drill hole in your hairy head."

Kaufmann backed off. "Hey, now look. I don't want any trouble with you guys. Just being friendly, is all. I'm just trying to help out. You know, you really shouldn't—"

The unarmed creature rushed him. The jewel-torch clattered to the floor and Kaufmann went flying. The corridor wall interrupted his flight with a sickening thud. The creature then picked him up like a limp rag and began to pummel him mercilessly.

The other creature went for the torch, scooped the thing up, and examined it. At length he looked over his shoulder and growled, "Don't kill it! Proconsul will want to interrogate!"

Kaufmann lay still on the floor, one arm at an anatomically improbable angle.

"Two-legged, hairy creature that talks. Fantastic! Where did it come from?"

"From this place, wherever."

"Look. It has red blood."

"I can see that, fool!"

"Can you also now see—*idiot*—that there is something more to this?"

The other regarded the torch again. "Perhaps so." It ran a sausagelike finger over the handle.

The unarmed creature pointed at Kaufmann.

"Come, we must report this. Bring creature." When the other gave no response: "That is my order!"

The other glared back. "I urinate on your orders. You have no authority over me."

"I have Proconsul's authority! I am his chief of staff. As captain of stronghold guard, you are technically under my command. Obey!"

"Slime-eating schemer! You backstabbed your way to power!"

The other smiled toothily. "I could have you shot." His hand was a blur as it slipped behind his breastplate, bringing forth a small pistol. He trained it on the captain. "I could shoot you right now."

"You are coward as well."

The chief of staff's smile faded. Slowly he put the pistol back into its hiding place. He brought back his hand to his side.

"Now make your move."

It was quiet. Both creatures remained motionless for several minutes.

The captain of the guard carefully unbent and relaxed. "This is foolish. I will fetch prisoner."

The chief of staff picked up the torch. Looking it over, he walked toward the opening. Just as he reached it he caught sight of what the captain was about to do.

The captain's pistol smoked and sputtered. A brief flame coughed from the end of the barrel. That was all. Dumbfounded, the captain stood looking at the useless weapon in his hand— briefly, until a dagger suddenly grew in his throat. He dropped the pistol, gurgled, and fell dead. Bright purple blood issued from the wound.

The chief of staff retrieved the knife and picked up the gun. He looked at one, then the other.

"Strange."

Throwing down the gun, he grabbed the human by the hair and dragged him back through the portal.

SIX
(Approximately)
MONTHS
(For Lack of
Better Word)
LATER

OVER THE PLAINS OF BARANTHE

HE PUSHED THE stick forward. The nose of the jet fighter dipped, allowing him to view the entirety of Castle Perilous atop its high citadel. It was as it always had been, a vast dark edifice of eye-defying complexity, a jumble of towers, turrets, bulwarks, and other fortifications, all ringed by concentric curtainwalls. The central keep soared into the clouds. The castle sat like a magistrate high on his bench, delivering judgments to the plains below and the snow-capped mountains beyond.

The castle belonged to him, as it had to his father, his father's father, his father's father's, etc., and all his forebears unto many generations. It was his home (one of them, at least), his freehold, and his fortress.

It was the biggest white elephant in the world. In several worlds, in fact.

But he loved the place.

He sent the plane into a wide banking circle around the castle and spent a good quarter hour inspecting it. As old as it was, the castle looked as though it had been built yesterday. No weathering discolored its stone, no mortar crumbled from its joints and cornices. It looked spanking new; in fact, it had been magically reconstructed a little less than a year before.

Without warning, the jet's single engine died with a whistling whine, and the lights on the instrument panel blinked, then went out.

"Infernal machine," he said irritably, shaking his head. He worked his fingers in complex patterns and muttered an incantation. The engine coughed once, roared to life, but faded seconds later. He worked his fingers again, chanting monotonously.

No use, the engine was dead. The jet dropped like a stone. He could have effected a levitation spell to keep it up, but that was hardly fun. Sighing, he waved his hand.

The jet disappeared, and was instantly replaced by a helicopter. He took the control bars, checked his counter-rotation, and put the ship into a steep dive.

He leveled off near the ground and hovered. The earth was blackened as if by a great fire. The copter bore down. Charred skeletons lay among the dust of the plain—the remains of the last army that had laid siege to Castle Perilous. The siege had been long and bitter, and the castle had almost fallen. But the besiegers had met a horrible end.

The helicopter's motor sputtered and choked.

"Damn!" He was dangerously close to the ground. He worked his fingers fast.

The aircraft that appeared around him was an eclectic meld of curving silver metal and clear, tear-shaped bubbles. It hummed and crackled. He looked over the controls—he had flown one of these only twice in his life—then gingerly put the tips of his fingers on the control panel. The craft shot toward the virginal blue sky with astonishing speed.

He leveled off at ten thousand feet, the castle still bulking hugely below him.

"Now to do what I came up here for," he said.

There was a computer terminal, of sorts, to his right. He studied it briefly, then punched in some data. A small screen next to the terminal lit up.

He was busy for several minutes. Then he looked up and searched the skies.

By the end of an hour, his neck hurt horribly and his eyes burned from reading instruments. It was hard work. The craft's engines had failed regularly every ten minutes or so, and had to be bolstered by complex levitation spells. The last of these was now fading rapidly.

"There you are!"

A fuzzy gray splotch floated against the bright sky. It looked like a defect in a camera lens, nebulous, out of focus. He headed the craft for it.

Worried that the engine might fail just at the wrong moment, he transformed the craft back to a jet fighter just before entry.

The sky didn't change color by much—it turned perhaps a shade lighter. Below sprawled an immense city cut by two rivers and outlined by a harbor. A long, thin finger of land, bristling with skyscrapers, ran between the rivers.

"I should have known. All roads lead to New York."

Smiling, he banked and turned toward Manhattan. It had been a long time.

Presently the radio sputtered and blurped.

"—Kennedy Air traffic control to unidentified military aircraft! Calling unidentified military aircraft! You are intruding in controlled air space! Come in!"

"Yes?"

"Unidentified aircraft—descend to fifteen hundred feet immediately! You are in a controlled air corridor! Acknowledge, please!"

"In a moment."

"Negative! Negative! You must—"

He snapped the radio off. This would never do. He suddenly realized how unprepared he was. Awkward, really.

The plane around him began to fade.

Of course. He had forgotten how inhospitable this world was to magic. Things were damned difficult here as far as the Arts were concerned. It was ironic. The jet didn't work very well back home because the universe of the castle was not amenable to mechanical contrivances, even conjured ones. Here, the jet worked fine, but its very existence was tenuous at best precisely because it was entirely a magical construct. He was getting the worst of both worlds.

That left him in somewhat of a pickle, one he should have smelled far off.

A simple shield spell protected him from most of the air blast when the jet finally faded out of existence, but even that began to wear off quickly. He stretched out his arms and legs and went into free-fall posture.

Plummeting toward the cold gray expanse of the East River, he decided that he would have to think of something very fast.

ELSEWHERE

"I'VE GOTTEN TO like the castle," Linda Barclay said as she munched a kosher dill. "But I still have really serious bouts of homesickness."

Sitting with his back against the tree under which he and Linda were enjoying a picnic lunch, Gene Ferraro bit into a cheese-laden cracker. "That's normal. I don't get so much homesick as bored with life here—I mean, in the castle. I'd like to get out into some of the more exciting worlds. Explore a little, you know."

"You're big for adventure. I'm not. I'm basically a homebody."

"And one of the most powerful sorceresses around."

"Only in the castle and in some of the magic-is-the-rule worlds. That's what I like about my life here, as opposed to back in the normal world. Magic is fun."

"Sure is. Normal world? No such thing. Our world is just one of many—and a pretty dreary one at that."

"It's so nice here." Linda looked out across the meadow. Bright sunlight brought out the delirious green of the grass, and a soft breeze stirred the budding tree above. It was fine, first-warm-day-of-spring weather.

"Yeah, but I'd still like to do some exploring." Gene looked over his shoulder. "Take that big house over there."

Linda looked at the top of the huge dome that barely showed above the crest of the hill to the right.

"Did you ever go over and take a good look at it?"

"No," she said.

"It's a monster. It obviously belongs to someone, as does this whole estate. But the place is deserted."

"I guess that's why everyone in the castle comes here to picnic. It's nice, and there's no one to bother you."

A bird chirped in a nearby tree. Wooly clouds plodded sheeplike across a blue-violet sky. Gene sighed and stretched out, hands laced together at the back of his head. A sword in its leather scabbard lay in the grass at his left side.

Linda said, "The way I hear, some of the castle's worlds are pretty depopulated, due to wars, plagues, and other nasty things."

Gene looked off into the sky. " 'The castle's worlds.' Say it that way, and it sounds like none of these places would exist if the castle didn't. I wonder."

"I never heard that. Kind of weird to think that our whole Earth existed just because Castle Perilous created a time warp, or whatever you call it."

"Spacetime warp. That's a scientific way of putting it. But Castle Perilous and everything about it has to do with magic, not science."

"Maybe the magic is just like science, only with different laws."

Gene shrugged. "Hard to say." He yawned. An insect buzzed about his head. He ignored it.

Linda stretched out one leg and adjusted her tights, then recrossed her legs. She echoed Gene's yawn. "Stop that, it's catching."

Gene feigned a loud, ripping snore.

Linda chuckled. "Maybe I should Z out, too. It was cold in the castle last night. I shivered all night long."

"Yeah, it does get cold sometimes," Gene murmured, eyes closed.

Linda looked off down the slope of the meadow.

"Gene?"

"Yeah."

"Have you ever seen a world with blue-skinned, muscle-bound creatures that wear green armor?"

Gene's right eye popped open. "Eh?"

"Look."

There were three of them, trooping in step up the hill. They were armed with swords and pistols, and all three wore backpacks.

Linda said, "Something tells me these guys don't live here."

"Right, they're definitely prospecting, checking the place out."

"Their armor's pretty."

"Yeah. Linda, does your magic work here?"

"I've never tried. I whipped the food up back in the castle." She looked off, her brow furrowed. "I think so." She made a motion with her hand. "Yeah, it works a little."

"Good. Then maybe those guns they're toting won't work." Gene's right hand went to the hilt of his sword. "Here they come, straight for us. Get ready to move fast."

At the last minute, the three strange creatures changed course to the left and marched by, their big webbed feet crushing the overgrown grass in purposeful steps. One of them regarded Gene and Linda coldly. The others looked straight ahead.

When they disappeared over the rise, Gene let go of his sword. "I wonder what that was all about."

Linda shrugged.

Gene snapped his fingers. "Wait a minute. I thought something was familiar about them! Don Kelly was telling me about how people have been seeing strange-looking new aliens around the castle. Blue-skinned, short, chunky guys, lots of them, usually going around in threes. They don't mix, keep to themselves. In fact, they're supposed to be kind of belligerent, if pressed. Those must be the ones."

"I wonder what their world is like."

Gene shook his head. "Each one of those guys must go two seventy-five, maybe three hundred pounds. At least. They look like good fighters. Too good."

"Do you think they're trouble?"

Gene shrugged. "No real reason to think they would be. They seem to mind their own business." He mulled it over. "Trouble is, they look like they have business."

Linda nodded. "Serious business."

They were silent for a while.

"Have we been here a year, yet?" Linda asked.

"Who's keeping track of time? Yeah, I guess."

Linda let out a long breath. "It seems shorter. Sometimes I still think this is all a dream."

"I know what you mean."

"A year ago I'm in Los Angeles, leading a normal life. I have a dull job, but I live near the beach in Santa Monica. It's okay, I guess. But I get depressed sometimes. A lot of the time. And I take a lot of pills. Then one day, when I'm feeling especially down, I open my closet and find that someone's torn out the back wall. I walk through and find this place that looks like the inside of a castle."

Gene broke in, "And the opening closes behind you, and you can't find a way back to your closet. And then you find there are all kinds of people in this castle, some good, some bad, some strange, some not. And the place is absolutely crazy, with doorways that lead to a million different worlds and universes—"

"Crazy isn't the word. Insane. Bonkers. Stark raving Looney-Toons."

"Never a dull moment. And there's even a king in this castle, by the name of Incarnadine." Gene sighed. "Yeah. Sounds familiar, except I came in by way of an odd doorway in a parking garage in downtown Pittsburgh, Pennsylvania. Of all places."

"Want to go back?"

"Huh? To our world? The good old USA, where I was born, like the song says?"

"Well, I meant the castle. But answer the question any way you want to."

"I dunno. The only thing that worries me is my parents. They must have given up hope by now."

"And mine."

"Sure wish there was a way to get a message back."

"Just a message?"

Gene nodded. "I like Castle Perilous. It's the ultimate trip, to use an expression out of the sixties."

"Let's trip back to the castle. I want to take a nap."

"At once, milady." Gene got to his feet and strapped on his sword.

Linda packed the wicker basket while Gene folded up the square of white linen they had used for a ground cloth. Then they both headed up the hill. The portal leading back to the castle stood among some trees just over the rise.

"I'm glad Snowclaw finally found a way back to his world," Gene said.

"Poor baby. He was practically dying from the heat."

"Yeah. He was in pretty bad shape. His fur was coming off in hunks."

"I miss him."

"So do I."

35TH AND MADISON

WHEN ALICE SUSSMAN heard the name of the author who was out at the front desk, she had to run to the files. Sure enough, the Spade Books backlist did show five titles published under the name of C. Wainwright Smithton. The titles hadn't been reprinted in years—decades.

She went to her "who's who" shelf and consulted several reference books. C. Wainwright Smithton was mentioned once or twice but information was sketchy. He was British, but emigrated here, wrote for the pulps in the thirties and forties, and published a few science fiction novels over the next two decades. His work had attracted much critical attention. One book referred to him as an "elusive genius."

As senior editor of science fiction and fantasy, it was Alice's duty to show hospitality to important writers who dropped in to visit—even if no one had ever heard of them.

"Very nice to meet you, Mr. Smithton," Alice said as she took the hand of the handsome white-haired gentleman in the checked overcoat. "You haven't been in to see us in quite some time."

"Oh, thirty years, I should say," Smithton said with a laugh. "I had a little trouble tracking down Spade Books, until I learned it had been bought out by the Bishop Publishing Galaxy."

"Spade Books still exists, Mr. Smithton, and it's doing fine. In fact, it's one of our strongest fiction lines. Won't you please come back to my office?''

Alice got him settled down with a cup of coffee on the couch in her office. She took the chair.

''What can we do for you, Mr. Smithton?''

''Oh, you can give me a book contract with an advance in six figures and one hundred percent of subsidiary rights.'' He grinned.

She grinned back. ''We'd love to see a proposal from you, Mr. Smithton. I'm sure you still have many fans out there who'd buy a book with your name on it. After all, you're one of the veteran writers in the field.''

''I'd be surprised if any of my old fans were still alive. I haven't had anything in print for years and years.''

''Yes, I know. We put out reissues of backlist titles every month. Your name has come up several times during our weekly editorial meetings. Uh . . . I'm sorry to say we haven't actually done anything about it yet, but—''

''Quite all right, Ms. Sussman. You couldn't have, anyway. The rights have long since reverted to me, and I was out of contact for so long. I'm not complaining. I've been out of the country for years. I just recently came back to New York to look into some financial affairs of mine. Unfortunately, things haven't worked out the way I'd expected, and, frankly . . . to use the modern idiom, I'm having cash-flow problems.''

Alice sat back and crossed her legs. ''I see. Well, we'd certainly like to do all we can to help. But of course—''

''I certainly don't expect a contract and a check today. A few days would be fine.''

Alice chuckled. ''That's asking a lot of the machinery around here. Generally it takes a few weeks to produce a contract, and another few weeks to grind out a check. Minimum.''

''I understand. Of course, I wouldn't expect special treatment just walking in here after thirty years—''

''Well, we'd like to do anything we can. We'll certainly look into reprinting some of your books, Mr. Smithton. I'm afraid I can't promise you anything at the moment, but—''

''You're very kind. What titles do you think would go these days?''

She teethed her lower lip. ''Well . . .''

''*Fortress Planet*, perhaps?''

"A classic, and one of my favorites," she lied whitely.

"You flatter me. *Blood Beast of the Demon Moon?*"

"Is that a horror number?"

"On the cusp. How about my fantasy, *Castle Ramthonodox?* Then, of course, there's my story collection, *Bright Comets and Other Obfuscations.*"

"Your work has been somewhat . . . neglected."

"I'm a has-been, you mean. Forgotten."

"Hardly," she said.

"Oh, it's true. And I never was prolific—"

"Unfortunately, quantity does count, as well as quality."

"—but it seems to me that I never did receive the last few royalty statements that were due."

Alice sat up. "Oh."

"I realize that thirty years is a long time, and your records . . ."

"Well, as a matter of fact, we do have a number of open files. Authors whose estates or heirs we can't locate. It may very well be—" She got up. "Won't you please wait here while I check with our accounting and legal departments?"

He cashed the check at a local bank and walked down Madison Avenue, heading for a little curio shop he used to know in the Lower East Side.

It had been tough persuading Alice Sussman—and the people in accounting—to cut him a royalty check this very day. The domination spell he had cast over the entire office had barely worked. Back home, everyone in the Bishop Publishing Galaxy would have been his willing slave. They all would have leaped out a ten-story window for him, single file. Here—forget it. The spell had only oiled the machinery a little bit. But it had worked. Done the job.

Well, there'd been a little give-and-take. Allie (at lunch she told him to call her that) had just about insisted that he submit an outline and sample chapters of a new book. Instead, over chicken lo mein, he spun out the plot of a sequel to *Fortress Planet,* quite off the top of his head, and she loved it. Well, the spell helped there a little, he had to admit. He hadn't written a word of fiction in years, and it must have been dreadful bilge he spilled out. Anyway, she'd offered a $14,000 advance, and he couldn't bring himself to refuse . . . Besides, he was stranded here and needed the money.

All in all, New York hadn't changed as much as he'd expected.

Numerous landmarks had disappeared, replaced by austere modern structures (he rather disliked the ubiquitous Bauhaus influence), but plenty of familiar sights were still left. He remembered this part of town well.

He began to notice that there were more distressed people milling about than he recalled seeing during the Great Depression. He passed a slovenly middle-aged woman who carried two great bags stuffed with debris. She was followed by an emaciated man in a filthy overcoat who seemed to have difficulty controlling his tongue. These and other unfortunates made up a good percentage of the sidewalk population.

Wetting a mental finger and putting it up into the psychic wind, he got a subtle but overriding sense of decay, of desuetude, of things coming apart. Pity. It was a good town, but it had once been a great town.

The curio shop was just where he remembered it to be. The shops around it had been long since boarded up. A derelict lay unconscious on the sidewalk a few doors away. In the other direction, a nervous-looking youth regarded him from the doorway of an abandoned storefront.

He entered to the soft tinkling of a bell. The place was stuffed to the ceiling with an amazing collection of miscellaneous junk, and he was astonished to recognize some pieces from years before. Obviously business had not been brisk. The place smelled of must, dust, and stale cigar smoke.

There was a sallow young man behind the counter. He did not smile when he asked, "Can I help you?"

"Is Mr. Trent in?"

"Why . . . yes, he is. Who shall I say is calling?"

"Carney. John Carney."

"One moment."

The young man slipped through a tattered curtain into a back room. There was a murmuring of voices. Then the young man returned.

"Mr. Trent will see you. This way."

He followed the young man into the back room. There, seated at an ancient rolltop desk, was a man in his early sixties wearing a gray suit of fashionable cut, along with a burgundy tie, a tailored shirt with a crisply starched collar, and oxblood loafers burnished to a mirror shine. Even in the dim light he cut an imposing figure. His hair was blond-white, his face thin. His eyes were ethereal blue disks over a thin blade of a nose. The mouth was small and precise. He regarded his visitor, eyes narrowing, straining for recognition. At length and with some astonishment, he said, "It *is* you."

"Hello, Trent."

Trent rose and offered his hand, nodding to the young man, who retreated through the curtain.

"Incarnadine," Trent said.

"Greetings, my long-lost brother," Incarnadine said in Haplan, the ancient tongue of the even more ancient tribe of the Haplodites. "How dost thee fare?"

"Thou art a sight for longing eyes," Trent answered. "Let's stick to English," he added, "or Alvin will start to wonder."

"Alvin looks okay. I'll bet he's heard many a strange thing back here."

"You're right. Have a seat." Trent dragged up a battered hardback chair.

Incarnadine sat. "It's been a long time."

"How did you ever manage to get here?" Trent said.

"Well, I've been meaning to crack the problem of the lost gateway for the longest time. Just recently it occurred to me that it could be one of the orbiting variety, the kind that don't necessarily stay inside the castle. So, I whipped up a flyer, searched the sky over the castle—and sure enough, there it was. Had a devil of a time chasing it down, though."

Trent lit a small brown cigar and puffed on it. "After thirty years, you decide to do this. Why?"

Incarnadine shrugged. "Any number of reasons. I miss New York . . . I miss this world. Lots of memories here." He smiled. "I thought you might have been stranded here when the spell stabilizing the gateway went on the fritz."

Trent looked hard at him. "You thought. And it takes you thirty years to decide to find out for sure?"

"What is time to a spawn of Castle Perilous? Sorry. Were you stranded? Are you?"

"You said yourself that you found the thing floating in the sky. Where did it leave out?"

"About three thousand feet over the East River."

Trent whistled. "And you were flying a magical contrivance?" He shook his head. "Tough spot to be in."

"Yeah. I'd really forgotten how hard it was to practice the Recondite Arts around here."

"What did you do?"

"Well, when the plane dissolved, I tried just about everything on the way down. At about three seconds to impact I tried a simple protection spell, and that saved the day. And my hide. I hit pretty hard, though. Fortunately, it was only a few strokes swimming to shore. I didn't get a drop on me."

"You were lucky. Still, I wonder why you risked it."

"We've been getting a lot of Guests from here in the past few years. Some of them would like a way back. I'm here to see if I can establish a permanent gateway again."

Trent's pale brow rose. "You did it for the Guests? Those losers?"

"It's the least I could do. I would have seen to it long ago, but—one, I've been busy. Two, most of the Guests like the castle and want to stay. But some don't, and I thought we owed them."

"How about all the rest?"

"Some have stabilized gateways. The others . . . well, someday I mean to do something for them, too."

"Most of those damn holes should have been plugged long ago," Trent said, scowling. "The place is nothing but a big, drafty fun house."

"Do you realize how much power it would take to keep all the aspects sealed up? Keeping the particularly nasty ones shut up uses enough already."

Trent chewed his cigar. "Well, I'm no expert on castle magic." He took the cigar out and tapped the ash into a ceramic tray. "So, you say it never occurred to you to find out what happened to me."

"I'm embarrassed to say that although I certainly wondered, I always thought you could take care of yourself in any situation."

"I see." Trent's smile formed a small crescent. "Actually it was years before I discovered the gateway had skedaddled. I like it here, as you knew."

"One of the reasons I never really worried about you."

"Well, you were never very solicitous of my welfare."

"Nor you of mine, Trent."

Trent grunted. "Let's be frank. We were rivals for the throne. Dad favored you, and that's all there was to it." Trent tapped out the cigar. "Look. We have lots to talk about. Let's drive out to my place. We'll have dinner, hash over old times. What do you say?"

"Sounds friendly."

"It is, Inky. Wait a minute." Trent got up, parted the curtain, and called out: "I'm leaving early. I'll drive. Get a cab home."

"Yes, Mr. Trent."

Trent unhooked a camel's-hair overcoat from an antique coat tree and pulled it on. "Let's go."

The car was a blue Mercedes sedan, meticulously polished and parked next to a sign that read ABSOLUTELY NO PARKING.

"Hell of a nice car to leave on the street," Incarnadine remarked.

"I have a few friends on the police force who look after it for me."

"Nice to have friends."

They got in and Trent started it up and headed east.

"I'm surprised you still have the old shop. Still need a front?"

"Nah, not really. You were very lucky to find me there. My employees open the place up maybe two, three days a week. Most of my business is strictly legitimate these days. Real estate, stocks, the usual. The shop's still a good write-off, though." He chuckled. "I've been depreciating the same inventory for decades."

"Still deal in art?"

"My old hobby. I own a gallery on the West Side. Keeps the creative juices flowing." Trent honked at a taxi that cut in front of him. "Tell me this, why the hell didn't you try to stabilize the aspect from the other side? Why did you risk coming through and getting stranded?"

"I tried everything I could think of back home, but nothing worked. Something's changed. The stresses between the two universes have shifted over the years. It's not the same. Probably why the old spell failed."

Trent nodded. "I see." He made a series of lefts and rights, then turned north on First Avenue.

They were in the midtown tunnel when Trent asked, "Do you think you can tunnel back?"

"I'm going to give it the old college try. If I flunk out . . . can you take on a new employee?"

ICE ISLAND

SNOWCLAW HAD BEEN kneeling all day on an ice floe, waiting for a huge sea animal called the *jhalrakk* to come within range of his harpoon. But the jhalrakk had other ideas. It was content to stay where it was, just out of reach, half submerged in the shallow icy waters of the inlet. It had been feeding all day, ingesting vast quantities of water and filtering out what was edible. Only when it had its fill would it move out to sea again, and maybe—just maybe—its course would take it near Snowy's position.

Snowclaw knew it was a big jhalrakk (the word was sort of a growl, done with a snap of the jaws). He'd wanted to bag a big one all his life. This might be his chance.

It was cold. It was always cold here; the perennial question was *how* cold. Today, it was *very* cold. Bone-freezing cold. You had to watch when you took a leak outside, so as not to wind up stuck to one end of a pisscicle. It was *cold*.

Snowclaw hadn't moved for a very long time. Slowly he brought his four-digited hand to his belly, where the fur was a little thinner and finer than that which covered the rest of him, but just as milk-white. Bone-white claws extruded from the ends of his fingers. He scratched carefully, exhaling.

His feet, which were huge and padded with thick spongelike

tissue at sole and heel, were cold. His left knee was cold. His butt was cold.

Damn, he thought. I'm *cold*.

He didn't know whether he'd be better off bagging the jhalrakk or not. If he did, he'd be all night gutting it, cutting it, and dragging the carcass back to his shack. And tomorrow would go to rendering blubber, seasoning hide, and doing a hundred different other things with all the products and by-products that jhalrakks produced. He didn't look forward to any of that; it was all hard work. He just might freeze if he had to stay outdoors any longer. On the other hand, if he didn't bag something soon, he would starve. But at least he wouldn't have to break his back doing all that damn work.

It had been a very lean hunting season. He needed a little luck, or he didn't know what he was going to do.

The jhalrakk suddenly began moving. Snowclaw tensed, his left hand coming up to grip the front of the harpoon's shaft, his right moving back along its length.

The jhalrakk was heading straight for the floe. Snowclaw rose to a crouch and brought the point of the harpoon in line with the sharp, spiny back of the jhalrakk as it cut through the water, steaming toward him like a great ship, the kind Snowclaw would spy far out to sea sometimes. The spine rose, revealing the broad rubbery expanse of the beast's flanks. Then the head came out of the water. Its six eyes seemed to focus right on Snowclaw. The beast's great maw opened, revealing row on row of needlelike teeth.

Snowclaw swallowed hard and ran his tongue across his frost-white fangs. He stood up.

Come on right at me, big fellow.

Snowclaw made his shot. The harpoon skidded off the blubbery flank of the jhalrakk and plopped into the water. Snowclaw grabbed the line but his numbed hands couldn't stop it until it had paid all the way out, pulling taut against the iron anchor spike which had been pounded into the ice. Snowy growled and pulled on the line, but the jhalrakk had run over it, and now the big animal was diving. The beast slid out of sight, disappearing into the frigid, blue-black depths of the inlet.

Big it was, the largest that Snowy had ever seen. The jhalrakk was now underneath the floe. Snowy prayed that it would stay submerged and pass on out to sea. But the way it had looked at him . . .

The floe lifted out of the water, tilting sharply to the right. Snowclaw threw himself flat and hung on to the iron spike.

The floe soon became almost vertical and seemed about to tip over. Snowy knew he was in for a dunking, anyway, so he let go and slid into the water, hoping that he could swim away before the huge slab of ice flipped over on him.

It didn't. Snowclaw surfaced and watched the massive ice island slide off to one side and slip back into the water edgewise. The jhalrakk appeared satisfied that it had done enough damage. With a mocking wave of its flukes, it moved off serenely toward the open sea.

Snowy couldn't recall ever hearing of a jhalrakk big enough to lift an ice floe; a good-size one could overturn a large boat, for sure. But a huge, weighty mass of ice? It was ridiculous.

He swam back to the floe and climbed painfully back up on the ice. The wind hit him, making his waterlogged hide feel like a suit of fire. He pulled in the line, only to discover that he'd lost his best harpoon. With a savage growl, he yanked out the spike and threw it and the line as far as he could out to sea.

Some time later, grumbling, cursing, and generally bad-mouthing the world and everything that crawled or swam or walked in it, Snowclaw waded through deep drifts on his way to the only really warm spot he knew. He hadn't thought he would ever go back, but he was at the end of his tether. Maybe the time he'd spent away had made him go soft. He was losing his touch. You couldn't have asked for a more perfect setup shot on that jhalrakk. And he'd missed. Blown it completely.

He was just about frozen through, and could barely move, his fur a stiff mat of ice. The wind was howling out of the north throwing light snow, and night was falling. He could barely see through the icy rime forming over the fur around his eyes.

He found the crevasse and the steps he'd cut out of the ice going down into it. Minding where he put his feet, he descended the treacherous staircase.

The mouth of the cave was only a few steps from the bottom of the stairway. He went in, and the temperature immediately rose a few degrees. A few more steps inside the cave brought a warm draft from within. It felt like heaven.

There was a Gothic arch at the end of the tunnel, passing him through to a stone-walled corridor.

He was back in Castle Perilous.

The first time he'd stumbled in here, he and his hairless buddy Gene had met up and trooped around together. They'd wandered through the damn place for weeks, hopelessly lost. But after a while they'd become seasoned Guests of the castle, acquiring a sixth sense that allowed them to navigate the vast edifice with a reasonable chance of at least finding a way to the lavatory.

He made a series of lefts and rights, moving through bare hallways lit by jewel-tipped light fixtures in their wrought-iron mounts.

At length he smelled food: human food, which ordinarily he found rather tasteless. But if he talked nice to the cooks, they would whip up something more to his liking. If Linda was around, she'd do it for him no questions asked.

He found the Queen's dining room and walked in. There were a number of hairless types—humans—at the table, his old friends among them.

"Snowclaw!"

Linda jumped up, ran over, and hugged him. He hugged back, careful not to crush the little human female, of whom he was greatly fond.

"Snowy, you're soaking wet!"

"Yeah, I been swimming."

Gene Ferraro thumped him on the back. "I *knew* you'd come back."

"You knew something I didn't," Snowclaw said. "Not that I didn't miss you, Gene, old buddy. How's it going?"

"Oh, been pretty quiet around here."

"Find a way back to your world yet?"

"Nope," Gene said. "Still working on it."

"That's too bad. We'll have to mount a search party. After all, you helped me find my aspect."

"It was nothing. Yours is one of the stable ones."

"So far. You know what they say, though. Any aspect can close up on you, anytime."

"Yeah, but I wouldn't worry about it."

Linda asked, "Why did you come back, Snowy?"

"Couldn't make it in the real world. I'm hungry."

Snowclaw scanned the table for anything he could eat. He grabbed a candle out of its sconce, dipped it into gooey white salad dressing, and took a bite. The thin man sitting in front of the empty sconce looked up and smiled bleakly at him.

"Sorry, pal," Snowclaw said. "Was that yours?"

"No, quite all right. You ought to try the silverware."

Gene said, "I'm glad you showed up, Snowy. I've been giving some thought to going exploring. Just picking an interesting aspect and heading off into it. Feel like going with me?"

"Sure, let's go. Just so it's someplace warm."

"I thought you didn't take to heat."

"I'm slowly becoming a convert to your way of thinking."

"Well, let me finish breakfast, and we'll scout around and see if we can find something interesting. Have a seat, Snowy."

Snowy said, "Linda, can I talk you into whipping up some grub for me?"

"Sure thing. What would you like?"

"Oh, the usual."

"You mean that fishmeal mush you like? The icky green stuff?"

"If it won't make you puke."

"Don't be silly. You have to eat the food your body needs. Hold on a minute."

Linda closed her eyes briefly, extending her right hand palm-down over the table. A large wooden bowl materialized under her hand. It was filled with icky green stuff.

"Thanks, Linda," Snowclaw said, taking the bowl and scooping out a gob of mush with his fingers. His fierce yellow eyes lit up as he sat down and began to eat in earnest.

"I don't know about you two running off like that," Linda said. "I'm going to worry about you."

"We'll be fine," Gene said, helping himself to more chicken a la king.

Snowclaw had sat down next to a chubby young man with a straggly beard who was staring at him with a mixture of awe and repugnance. Snowclaw caught his stare.

"Something bothering you, friend?"

"Huh?" The young man's face turned a shade paler. "No! Not a thing. Really. Uh . . ."

Linda intervened with, "Snowy, this is Barnaby Walsh. He's a new Guest. Barnaby, I'd like you to meet our friend, Snowclaw."

"A pleasure to meet you, Mr. Snowclaw."

"Same here. Pass that salt, would you?"

"Certainly. Here you are."

"Thanks."

Linda said, "Barnaby is an American, just like us."

"That's real nice."

"Uh . . ." Barnaby smiled sheepishly. "I don't understand. I mean, obviously Mr. Snowclaw is . . . well, he's not a human being. But I can understand him perfectly. He even sounds American! But how could that be?"

"The translation spell," Gene said.

"The what?"

"It's operative throughout the entire castle. It's a magic spell that gives you an instantaneous running translation of any language. Snowy's speaking in his own tongue, just like everybody else here. Take Mr. Hoffmann over there, for example. He's German, and he speaks no English. Right, Mr. Hoffmann?"

"That's right."

"I don't get it," Walsh said. "He just spoke English."

"No, he didn't. He said it in German. Didn't you, Mr. Hoffmann?"

"*Ja.*"

"Well, I heard it that time," Walsh said.

"You can turn the translation off if you want to. For instance, just listen to the sound of Snowy's voice for a while. He grunts and barks and growls, but you understand him perfectly."

"But how?"

"It's magic!" everyone at the table chorused. Then they all laughed, except Walsh.

"I think I'm going insane," Walsh said, covering his face with his chubby hands.

Linda reached out a hand. "Now, Barnaby, don't lose it. Come on. If I could adjust, so can you. I was in worse shape than you when I wandered in here."

"It's just all so fantastic. So unbelievable."

"It's real. Just go with it. Don't fight it. It's fun, mostly. Things can get a little dangerous sometimes, but magic is the rule here. Anything goes."

"Do you really think . . ." Barnaby steadied himself with a gulp of coffee. "Will I really develop magic powers?"

"Everyone who becomes a Guest does. Castle Perilous is like a big dynamo, spinning off this fantastic energy. We act sort of like conductors. But each person's powers are unique. Everyone can do something different."

"You mean I might not be able to materialize things, like you, but I'll get some other power?"

"Right. For instance, Snowy here can teleport like a champ."

"Really? No kidding."

Snowclaw nodded. "Yeah, I can zip all over the damn place just by thinking about it."

"And Gene is the greatest swordsman in this and a few other worlds."

"Zat is becawse ah am French."

"You're French?"

"Of course. Why else would ah have zis ridiculous accent, eh?"

"French accents are not necessarily ridiculous," said a gentleman named DuQuesne. "I wish you could hear what most Americans sound like when they try to speak French."

"Whoops, looks like I put my foot in it again," Gene said. "Sorry, Monsieur DuQuesne."

M. DuQuesne laughed. "I was teasing you, Gene."

"Well, I don't mean to go treading on nationalist feelings. I mean, we've all got—" Gene caught sight of something and trailed off.

He was staring over Linda's head. Linda turned to see three blue-skinned creatures enter the dining room and stop to survey it imperiously. They could have been the same three who had shown up on the picnic grounds.

They sauntered over to the table. One of them looked over the wide selection of comestibles spread from one end of the table to the other.

"Scavenger leavings," it said with disgust. "Garbage."

No one argued with the creature.

The middle one had picked up a turkey leg to sniff. The creature tossed the thing over its shoulder contemptuously.

"If you speak to the cook," Gene suggested to the first creature, "I'm sure you'll be taken care of."

The creature didn't answer. It stalked the length of the long table, sizing everyone up. It stopped at a place opposite Gene and stood arms akimbo, glaring, flashing its gleaming teeth. "What if I think your cook is garbage as well?"

"Then you'll starve, pal." Gene shrugged. "Those are the breaks."

"Breaks?" The creature's head turned slightly to one side, as if giving ear to an unseen interpreter. Then it nodded. "Understand.

Yes. Luck. You are lucky I am under orders. I will not kill you now. But I might take some pleasure kicking your miserable carcass about this room.''

"You'll take pleasure in this first, friend," Gene said, laying a hand on the hilt of his sword. His heart was jumping into his mouth as he said it.

"That would give me immense pleasure.''

"Suits me," Gene said. "And now suits me as well as later.''

The creature smiled the wickedest, toothiest smile Gene had ever seen or could ever have imagined. "You are brave. Surprising, inasmuch as your race is so cravenly peaceful.''

Gene laughed. "He don't know humans very well, do he?''

Nobody else laughed.

"Gene . . .'' Linda's warning was also a plea.

"Reconsidering," the creature said, "it might be worth being court-martialed to see this hovel tastefully decorated with your entrails—if you have any left after I am finished with you.''

"Well, there's only one way to find out, big fella.''

Snowclaw stood up. He towered at least two feet over the creature. "You're in my light, Blueface." Snowclaw placed a hand flat against the creature's shiny green breastplate and shoved. The creature went staggering backward but managed to stay on his feet.

Gene gulped uncomfortably. Any other living thing would have gone crashing into the wall.

The three intruders drew their swords almost in unison. Gene jumped up and followed suit, as did a number of armed males at the table. Snowclaw snarled and leaped toward the first creature, coming to a karate fighting stance, milky claws at their maximum extension.

"Halt!''

The voice had come from the arched entrance to the dining hall. There stood another blue-skinned creature, scowling in the direction of the one Snowclaw had shoved.

The first creature came to attention with its sword at present-arms. The others followed suit.

"There will be none of this," the creature at the door said.

"Yes, Squad Leader," the first creature acknowledged.

"You will report back to headquarters immediately. Consider yourself under arrest.''

"Yes, Squad Leader.''

"Go.''

The three soldiers left. The squad leader lingered at the doorway for a moment, its cold eyes taking the measure of the room and the beings contained therein. Then, abruptly, it turned and marched off.

Everybody breathed again.

"Gene, I don't believe you did that." Linda rolled her eyes and put her hands to her head.

Gene looked unhappy. "It wasn't me, it was the magic. This castle turns me into a cross between John Wayne and Cyrano de Bergerac, and something compels me to act out the role. Besides, that guy was getting on my nerves."

"Yeah, they're kinda pushy, aren't they?" Snowclaw said.

"What *were* those . . . things?" Barnaby Walsh asked, his face the color of Chinese bean curd.

"I don't know what you'd call them," Gene said. " 'Blueface' is as good as anything."

"Where do they come from?"

Gene shrugged. "One aspect or another."

"I've never seen them before," Hoffmann said. "But I've heard other Guests mention seeing them."

"Still want to go exploring, Gene?" Snowclaw asked.

Gene frowned and shook his head. "Not until we find out what these blue guys are up to."

"Goody, goody. I hope there's a rip-roaring fight in it."

Barnaby Walsh gave Snowclaw a look of dismay.

"I could use a good fight," Snowclaw told him. "I really like it when the fur flies and the guts go spilling all over the place." Snowy licked a gob of mush from his thin pink lips. "Kinda pretty."

Walsh belched. "Excuse me," he said, getting up from the table. "I don't feel quite—" He riffed again, tottering away.

"Was it something I said?" Snowclaw asked.

LONG ISLAND

TRENT'S HOUSE WAS of dark red brick with black wood trim, and stood on wooded grounds somewhere in the wilds of Nassau County, sea gulls pinwheeling in the sky above it. The interior was tastefully and expensively appointed. An accelerated course in the history of modern painting covered the walls, and various avant-garde sculptures graced tabletops and display pedestals. The furnishings were mostly modern, with dashes of tradition for flavor.

Trent's study was book-lined and warm, a cheery fire going in the hearth.

"So, you say you've had some trouble up at the old place recently?"

Incarnadine took the glass of sherry from Trent and nodded. "It was a full-scale siege. Nearly successful, too."

"Really? Who was it?"

"Vorn."

"Prince Vorn of the Hunran Empire?" Trent seated himself in the leather easy chair opposite Incarnadine's. "I wouldn't have thought Castle Perilous was worth the bother."

"He didn't think so, either. Melydia worked her business on him, and he followed her like a lost, hungry puppy."

"Amazing. Melydia, huh? She still has it in for you. Hell's fury has nothing on that woman."

"Had."

Trent's eyebrow's rose. "Dead?"

"In a sense. She got to the Spell Stone, and—"

"Gods!"

Incarnadine smiled. "Yes, she finally figured it out. She got to it, somehow, and unraveled the transmogrification spell."

"But . . ." Trent was appalled. "That could have meant the end of everything."

"Almost did."

Trent waited. "Well, for crying out loud, tell me what happened!"

"It's a long story. She messed up just enough to give me an edge. I did a little research, and found a good handle by which I could recast the spell almost immediately."

"That must have taken some doing. But then, you must have seen . . . it. However momentarily."

"Oh, yes. I saw it."

Trent sat back. "Ramthonodox," he murmured.

"The Ancient Beast, the Primal Demon. Ramthonodox, Hell-spawned enemy of man. Old Brimstone Breath himself."

"It must have been an awful sight, in the true sense. Inspiring awe."

"It was. It did."

"Yet," Trent went on, "perhaps thrilling, in some strange, subliminal way?"

Incarnadine considered it. "I wasn't very thrilled at the time."

"Not the tiniest bit? The primal force, the unlimited power of it—"

"Maybe a little. Evil has its attractions. But pure evil is a little heady even for the likes of us. Besides, evil really isn't a force, is it? It's more like entropy; the undoing of things."

"Depends on your philosophical point of view, I suppose. Still, it must have been . . . stimulating, in any event." Trent took a sip of whiskey. "But you managed to fix up the spell and reconstitute the castle. So Castle Perilous is still a place to hang your hat in, not a demon running around loose."

"Right. I'm here, aren't I?"

"So you are. What about Vorn and his minions—I presume he brought his army with him, and not just an overnight bag?"

"There was a slight but unavoidable delay in recasting the transmogrification spell."

"Oh, I'll bet," Trent said, grinning malevolently.

"Ramthonodox had a good time out there on the plains. Nothing left of Vorn or . . . well, there wasn't much left of anything after old Rammy was through."

Trent shook his head slowly. "And Melydia?"

"Strangest thing. After it was all over, I heard her voice in the castle. Can't exactly figure out what happened to her. Got caught up in the spell somehow."

"Justice. The poetic kind, too."

"Perhaps."

"Well." Trent smiled at his brother. "It's nice to see you again, Inky."

"You haven't called me that in . . . hell, I hate to think how long."

"About a century and a half? Longer."

"Not since you and I were at university," Incarnadine said.

"Which one? The one in Hunra, where we learned magic, or at Cambridge, where we read natural philosophy?"

"I never liked Hunra much, I must say."

"Neither did I. It was a good thing Dad was so keen on us learning the ways of nonmagic universes."

"Of which this one is the most nonmagical," Incarnadine said.

"Well, Dad had a fondness for Earth generally, and for western European culture specifically."

"Not surprising, since this culture bears some resemblance to our own. He once told me he spent some time in England. That's why he gave us all English names, he said." Incarnadine sampled the sherry, then continued, "I've always thought he must have been Merlin."

"You think?" Trent thought it over. "Fantastic. I'd never considered it. But when you consider the time frame—" He shrugged it off. "Dad never did tell us how old he was, and I'm not particularly interested in researching his exploits."

There was a pause as Incarnadine stared into the fire. Then he asked, "Do you still hate me, Trent?"

"Whatever led you to believe I hated you?"

"Just a feeling."

Trent looked away. "I don't hate you, Inky. You did come between me and my ambitions . . . once." He sighed. "But that was centuries ago. I'm happy here. You can see that. The gateway disappeared, and I didn't know it for five years. I never planned on going back, you see.''

Incarnadine nodded. "But when I die?"

"Do you plan on dying soon?"

"No."

"Well? Yes, I suppose I'm next in line for the succession, but I'm not interested. If I were—" Trent grinned cordially. "—I'd simply kill you now."

"You could, I suppose. Easily. No one knows I'm here. Officially I don't exist in this world."

Trent got up and went to the bar. "Forget it. I've no interest in taking possession of a huge, drafty old castle that's a cross between a carnival sideshow and a sci fi movie." He made himself another whiskey and soda. "Besides, I own my share of useless real estate up in the Bronx. At least I can hire a guy to torch an abandoned apartment building."

Trent's oriental servant opened the door and poked his head in. "Dinner, sir," he said.

"Thank you, Phan," Trent answered as the door closed, then downed his drink in three swallows. "Well, shall we go in and eat?"

Dinner was superb, and mostly silent. There did not seem to be much more to talk about until coffee was served.

"Good food," Incarnadine said.

"Phan does a good job. He was raised in a French Catholic mission in Phnom Penh—learned to cook Parisian."

"Best *coq au vin* I've ever had."

"I'll tell him." Trent lit a cigar and puffed thoughtfully. "When was the last time you heard from anyone else in the family?"

"Oh, not so long ago. Dorcas dropped in a while back."

"How is our dear elder sister? She still married to that fat potentate who copulates with animals?"

"Nobody ever approves of in-laws. Besides, it's a religious ritual, common in his land."

"Disgusting. How about Ferne?"

"She hasn't shown up in years. I fear for her. She was a wild one."

"Oh, I've a notion Ferne's okay . . . somewhere. And Deems?"

"Deems is still King of Albion, and loves it. He'll never leave the place. I don't blame him, it's pretty nice." Incarnadine drank the last of his coffee and sat back. "Then there's Uncle Jarlath—"

"To hell with Uncle Jarlath and the rest of the fossils. I couldn't care less."

"In that case, that's all the news from back home. What's new with you? Is there a woman in your life? Or women?"

"Forgive me, Inky, but I don't feel like exchanging warm personal data with you just now. If you don't mind."

"Of course."

"I'm sorry. I didn't even ask about your current family. Uh, you do have one, don't you?"

"They're fine."

"What's the new one's name? I mean the wife."

"Zafra."

"Hmm. Sounds very nice."

"She is."

Another lull occurred before Trent said, "Where are you staying, Inky?"

"Hotel. I'm looking for an apartment in the city."

"In Manhattan? You'll be lucky to get on a five-year waiting list for anything reasonable. Unless you're talking about spending big money."

"I'm somewhat financially embarrassed at the moment."

Trent smirked. "Tricky getting used to a hard-physics world again, isn't it?"

"Very. The credit card I materialized to pay for the hotel disappeared a microsecond after I put it back in my wallet—which vanished not very much later."

Trent's look was detached, analytical. "If you're that far along already, maybe I would be taking a big risk trying to knock you off right here and now." Then the smile resumed. "Just kidding, brother."

Incarnadine's hand came up from beneath the table gripping a large revolver. "Just in case you're not," he said. "This won't last a minute, but a second is all it would take."

Trent laughed. "One thing I would never, never want to do, Inky, is underestimate you." Then he suddenly frowned in mock indignation. "Really, Inky, that was uncalled for."

"Sorry." The gun disappeared. "You've been making what I took to be veiled threats all afternoon. Sorry if I've misinterpreted."

"You have. I should apologize, though. Inky, I don't want to hurt you, or get in your way . . . or do anything, really, but continue leading my life. All I ask is that you leave me alone."

"That is not an unreasonable request," Incarnadine said. "I might ask the same of you."

"Then let's bury the hatchet. Let's agree to disagree, live and let live, and all the rest of that stuff."

"Let's." Incarnadine rose from the table. Trent did not.

"Inky, I've been meaning to comment—your disguise is pretty good. It's not magic, but it's a fair makeup job. How did you do it?"

"I went into a costume shop, bought some stage makeup, this wig, and the moustache. A few age lines here and there, a touch of pancake . . ." He shrugged. "Yours *is* magic, I suppose."

Trent snapped his fingers and the years melted away in an instant. Incarnadine beheld Trent as he had looked the last time they had seen each other, sometime in the late 1950s.

"Pretty neat," Incarnadine remarked. "You seem to have no trouble with the Arts here."

Trent shook his head. "Rudimentary stuff."

"Effective, though. I should ask you to give me lessons. But now, Trent, I have to go."

"Phan will drive you back to New York."

"I wouldn't think of it. Can you call me a cab?"

"We're out pretty far, Inky. Phan can run you into Great Neck, though, and you can get a train for the city."

"That suits me."

"It's been nice."

"Goodbye, Trent."

"And keep in touch," Trent added, smiling pleasantly.

WILMERDING, PENNSYLVANIA

OHMYGAWD. SATURDAY NIGHT and no date. Jesus, Mary, and Joseph. Invoking all deities, great and small.

Sheila turned the water in the tub on and yanked up the thingee on the spigot that made the water come out of the shower head.

Oh Jesus H. Christ on the proverbial crutch. Sorry, sorry, don't mean to offend any supernatural personages. Can't afford that, not with the way things have been going. Oh hell.

She looked in the mirror. Same face. It doesn't go away, doesn't change. Still Sheila. Who did you expect?

Another Sa-tur-day night and I AIN'T got no-BOD-y . . . da da da da da dee dee dum dum DUM—

She let the ratty old robe drop and looked at herself. Her breasts seemed to sag just a little lower than they did the last time she'd looked at them. Mygawd, could this process be taking place *overnight?* Did they go—plop—just like that? Or was it her imagination?

She couldn't quite see her butt, though she knew she was okay in that department, at least. Thank heaven for small favors. She wasn't going completely to pot. Her weight was fine.

Oh, for Christ's sake, stop this damn fixation about the body, okay? So you're getting older. It's inevitable. Completely natural process. Everything's fine. Just . . . fine. So you've had two horrible marriages. Great. So you hate your job. Okay, so you hate the goddamn world. So what? That's life, kid.

The bathroom filled with steam and her image grew misty and faded. Faded away.

She wiped the mirror with two fingers and saw one green eye peeking back at her. Still there, Sheila?

Still there.

She got in and the water was a little hot, so she adjusted it. She let the spray sting her until it cooled down, perversely enjoying the discomfort.

No date. No men in her life. No men anywhere. No guys at work she wanted to *work* with, let alone go out with. The bar scene was deadly. 99.99999 percent of the men she *did* meet were: (1) pinheads; (2) multiple-attempt losers (like herself!); or (3) married. Most of them, it seemed, were (3). Why was she always meeting married men she liked? Some weird psychological thing, no doubt.

She poured a cold gob of Herbal Essence into her hand, slapped the stuff on her head, and smooshed it around until it lathered.

Two disastrous marriages. Actually the latest had been the worst. Frank was . . . still *is,* from all reports . . . nuts. He had problems; *serious* problems. Her lawyer files, he gets the papers at work, and what does he do? He leaves work, goes straight to the house, breaks in (the locks had all been changed), and proceeds to trash the place from top to bottom. All the furniture, slashed, ripped, broken apart. Carpeting slit down the middle with a linoleum cutter. Dishes smashed, the stereo stomped on and wrecked, the bed . . . the *bed,* for Christ's sake, a complete shambles. The crazy bastard didn't miss a piece of communal property. Property settlement! Hah! What property?

What if she had been home at the time? Ohmygawd. He would have killed her.

Sure, she got a judgment against him for the damages, but who knew when he'd pay up, if ever? The schmuck was broke. Meanwhile, she had a house full of broken junk, this monster mortgage, a shit job at Mellon Bank, and she was stuck in Wilmerding.

Wilmerding.

Wilmer . . . *ding.*

She rinsed, then poured out another gob of goop and lathered again. Gonna wash that jerk right outta my . . . yeah, right.

No date. So we bathe, *madame,* and we brush on a little

Clinique, and spritz on a touch of . . . oh, what would be good for tonight?—some cheap smelly crap, real whory stuff, and then, *mesdames et messieurs*, we go down to Chauncey's and watch the pretty lights and listen to the music and nurse a glass of Chablis until some insurance underwriter sidles up and asks us to dance to a disco (migraine-inducing rhythm track overlaid) redub of an old Beatles number. . . .

A sudden cold blast of air hit her, and she began to shiver. Her heart thumped against her breastbone. *Somebody had come in! Somebody had opened the bathroom door!*

But the draft was coming from the wrong direction, from the wall. Suds-blind, she reached out.

And there was no wall. She felt the shower curtain to make sure that she hadn't gotten turned around somehow. No! But . . . there was nothing but empty space to her right, where the side of the one-piece molded-fiberglass tub and the section of water-stained wall above it should have been. She stretched her arm and swung it in a wide arc. Nothing! She was freezing. She bent and reached out as far as she could.

She slipped, stumbled, and fell onto a hard cold floor.

There came a sudden quiet.

Soap burning her eyes, she struggled to her feet. She wiped and wiped at her face but stuff wouldn't get out of her eyes and she yelled in pain.

After an agonizing few moments she could see a tiny bit.

What the hell—?

She was standing in a room with walls of stone and a ceiling like a church or something. There was a table and two chairs, and cold fireplace, and a sort of couch. Nothing else. She was standing on a gray stone floor, naked, dripping wet, and covered with suds. And freezing to death.

She whirled. She stood about two feet from a blank stone wall. The shower, the water . . . her house, were gone. Gone.

Slowly she turned around, her soap-reddened eyes in a zombie stare.

Gone. One second she was . . . and then she . . .

She screamed. But it didn't do any good. Nothing changed. She was still naked, cold, wet, scared, and in a situation she didn't understand.

She screamed again, then decided not to do it a third time.

She searched the wall for any sign of an opening, a hole, a seam, a crack, something, anything—any trace of a connection or bridge or transition between her existence of not half a minute ago and her existence now. There was nothing. The wall was as solid and as unyielding as stone walls rightly should be. She searched again. No change; no bathtub, no bathroom, no house, no Wilmerding. This was someplace else. Someplace else entirely.

There was a doorway to her right and she approached it cautiously, her sudsy feet precarious on wet, slippery stone. She poked her head out into a hallway, looked one way, then the other. Nothing but a corridor lit only by a few windows up and down it.

Grimacing from the chill and hugging her rib cage, she went out into the hall and trotted to the nearest window.

She was in a church, a cathedral, or some huge Gothic stone edifice. She could see a forest outside, and mountains. It was a bright day. Last time she had looked outside, it was a dark winter Saturday night. Now it was broad daylight. Different place, different time.

A castle—yes, the building looked more like a castle. A huge one, from what she could see. The window must have been forty stories off the ground.

She was cold. She toddled off down the hallway, at length discovering a huge wooden door to the left. She tried the wrought-iron handle; the door wouldn't budge. She passed another window and came to a dead halt, as if hitting an invisible barrier. No, she couldn't have seen what she thought she'd seen. She backtracked and looked out.

Yes, she'd seen it. There was a desert out there, vast and dry and empty. A molten sun beat down on endless salt flats, scorched and featureless, upon which there grew not a weed, nor a blade of grass.

She went back to the first window. The forest—as lush and green as before—was still out there, as were the glorious snow-capped mountains that rose in the distance.

She returned to the second window and stared out, forgetting her nudity, forgetting herself.

Presently the drying soap began to itch, and she turned away and continued down the hall. She again grew aware that she was cold.

"Help," she called, as calmly as possible. "Somebody help me, please."

No one answered. She came to a casement window with panes of leaded glass, but declined to look out. She called out again, and again no answer came.

She tried another door, then another. The third was unlocked, and she peeked in.

It was a bedroom. The bed was huge and looked quite comfortable, covered with blankets and quilts and decorated pillows. There were night tables on either side which held lamps, and a big wooden chest lay at the foot of the bed. A tall pine wardrobe stood off to the right, and a dressing table lay near the huge open window. She went to the window and looked out.

The castle spread out endlessly beneath her, a tumult of walls and towers and courtyards and buildings. Beyond the farthest wall there was a sheer drop and then a wide plain. On the horizon, black mountains hulked against the sky like storm clouds.

The window had thick velvet curtains which she untied and let fall. The room darkened. She checked the door and found that it had an old-fashioned lock turned by a huge old-fashioned key. She twisted the key until she heard a click, then ran for the bed. She tore the covers down and slipped in. The sheets had been warmed by the sun, and she luxuriated in the comfort of it, sighing with relief.

She looked around the room. Ohmygawd, what a place to spend a Saturday night. Naked—and no goddamn date!

She pulled the covers over her head.

CASTLE KEEP—WEST WING

GENE, LINDA, AND Snowclaw approached the door to Gene's room.

"I think we should make some systematic effort to search for their portal," Gene was saying. "Find out where they're coming from."

"Track 'em," Snowclaw said.

"Yeah, that's it. We follow a couple of them. Eventually they'll go back to their world and we'll at least know—oh, damn it. The maid must have locked my door. I don't have my key, either."

Linda asked, "Want me to materialize it?"

"Yeah, sure."

A key appeared in Linda's hand. "Is this it?"

"We'll find out."

Gene fit the oversize key into the keyhole and turned it. The lock clicked open. "Anyway, we have to keep a close watch on them, that's for sure," he continued, shouldering the door open and going in. He stopped in his tracks when he saw the naked woman dash away from the door and dive into the bed.

Linda bumped into him, then saw the strange female in Gene's bed.

"Oh, excuse me," Linda said, then turned and left.

The woman was peeking over the covers, eyes as round as

half-dollars. Gene stood there gawking for a moment. Then he called over his shoulder, "Linda? Hey, wait—"

Snowclaw came in, and the woman shrieked and disappeared under the sheets.

Gene said, "Uh, don't be afraid. He won't hurt you."

"Who's your new friend, Gene?" Snowclaw asked.

"Never saw her before. Uh, miss—?"

There came a frightened mewling from beneath the covers.

Gene laughed. "You know, that's a line right out of an old Bela Lugosi movie. 'Do not be afraid. He will not hurt you.' Snowclaw, do you mind leaving the room? I think I can handle this."

"I gotta find a room for myself, anyway. Darned if I know how I'll ever get used to sleeping on those soft bouncy things you humans like. See you later."

Snowclaw left.

"Uh, miss? Or ms., or whatever. You can come out now."

"I don't have any clothes!"

"Yeah. I'm aware of that. Uh, I mean, you can *look* out, if you want."

"Oh my God. Oh my God."

"Now, calm down. Take it easy."

She was a redhead with green eyes. Pretty, too.

"He's gone," Gene said.

"What . . . *was* that?" Sheila asked in wide-eyed wonder.

"I don't know the name Snowclaw's species goes by, but obviously they're humanoid, intelligent, and probably descended from ursine stock rather than anthropoids, like we are."

"Huh?"

"Bears. Polar bears."

"Oh. He didn't look much like a bear."

"No, not much. Looks ten times more ferocious."

"Oh my God."

"I'm Gene Ferraro."

"Huh? Oh. Sheila Jankowski."

"Hi, Sheila. You want some clothes?"

"Yes. Yes, please! Thank you."

Gene went to the wardrobe, opened it, and rooted. "Here's a tunic that's a little too small for me. It's just a one-piece thing. Linda can whip up a nice outfit for you anytime. I'll be in the john, there, so you can dress." He threw the garment on the bed.

When he came out of the bathroom, she was dressed and standing by the window looking at him sheepishly, apprehensively.

"I'm sorry I messed your bed up," she said. "Sorry I used your room. But, you see, I didn't know—"

"I don't mind in the slightest," Gene said.

"I heard you at the door," she said, "and I ran to see if I could bolt it. I . . . I didn't know—"

"Forget it. You're probably confused, right? You're probably wondering what the hell this place is, and what you're doing here, and why the hell I'm wearing something out of a bad old Tony Curtis movie—you know, the ones where he strikes a heroic pose and says, 'Yonder is da castle of my fodder.' Right?"

"Well, what you're wearing looks . . . interesting."

Gene rapped a knuckle against the leather cuirass that covered his chest. "Not much protection in a swordfight," he said, "but chain mail's too heavy and armor is ridiculous. I like to be able to move."

"Do you get a lot of use out of that?" she asked, pointing at his broadsword.

"It's saved my life any number of times."

"I see." She didn't see at all. Not at all.

Gene grinned. "Welcome to Castle Perilous."

164 East 64th Street

He had bought a color TV set to substitute as a computer CRT screen because of the sound capability. The set was nominally of American manufacture, though most of the parts bore oriental symbols. Lots of things had changed in this country.

He reattached the back of the set, tightening the screws a few turns. The adjustments he had made were minor, but necessary. He turned the set around on the table and sat back.

He began the incantation in a low monotone, then modulated to a wavering chant. As he did this he performed accompanying hand gestures. The screen began to form vague images. He continued the recitation until the screen went blank again.

"Damn."

His fingers went to the keyboard of the computer terminal and punched a few keys. A table of numbers appeared on the screen and he consulted it.

"More nearer A-flat than A-natural," he muttered.

He picked up a small plastic disk, about the circumference of which a number of small holes had been punched. He put the device to his lips and blew. A musical note sounded.

"That's more like it." He hummed a note in tune with the one that the pitch pipe had emitted. "Yes."

He began the incantation again, this time in a slightly altered tonality. The CRT screen came to life with a flurry of random images, fleetingly visible, along with accompanying sounds. In time, the images congealed into a scene.

The angle of sight was high, looking down on a large bed. A man and a woman lay in it, the man half sitting, half reclining, bending over the woman, who lay with both legs dangling over the high edge of the bed. The man was dressed in kingly robes, she in a maidservant's gown and cap. The man nuzzled her neck as he fumbled with the ties of her bodice.

"Deems? Sorry to bother you—"

"What!" The man sat up suddenly. The woman squealed, jumped up, and ran off-screen.

"Who calls?"

"Up here, Deems. To your left."

The man looked first to the right, confusedly, then to the left. Then he tilted his head up and peered straight out from the screen.

"Incarnadine! What the devil—?" He exhaled and rubbed his forehead, looking down. "Gods! You gave me a terrible start, Inky old boy."

"Sorry, Deems. I realize it's an awkward moment to reach you."

"Devil of a time. A man's hardly more vulnerable when he's dallying with a chambermaid." He chuckled. "I'm only relieved it was you instead of—" He looked about conspiratorially; then, in a whisper: "—instead of She-Who-Must-Be-Propitiated." Winking slyly he added, "If you know who I mean."

"How is . . . Flaminia?"

Deems looked pained. "Healthy as an ox, I'm sad to report. She scrutinizes my every move, hides the liquor, keeps a tight fist on my finances, and complains that I don't pay enough attention to her."

"I'm sorry for you, Deems."

"Don't be, old boy. Otherwise, things are fine."

"How are things in fair Albion?"

"Middling indifferent. The northern barbarians threaten; the nobles carp about high taxes; the peasants squawk about ruinous quitrents; the royal treasury is just about depleted; trade imbalances are draining gold away from the country like shit through a sewer pipe—" He grinned broadly. "Same old story. How goes it with you? Where are you calling from, by the way?"

"New York."

Deems was impressed. "How did you ever find the portal?"

"It took some doing. About six months of trying different things."

"Well, congratulations. How is the place? Did they ever get that global war settled?"

"Which one? There have been two of them in this century."

"Oh. Well, I forget just who the major combatants were. Actually I never cared much for that world."

"It's lost a lot of its charm in recent years," Incarnadine said.

"A shame. You're rather fond of the place, aren't you?" Without waiting for an answer, he went on to ask, "I say, is Trent still living there?"

"Yes, I found him, at the same location, in fact."

"Well, that's . . . good, I suppose. Hm. All this time and not a word from him."

"He seems totally uninterested in maintaining any family ties."

"I thought as much," Deems said, shaking his head disapprovingly. "A contrary bastard, that one. Always was."

Deems' image began to waver. Incarnadine made a few quick hand passes to correct the interference.

"What's wrong? Are you breaking off?"

"No," Incarnadine said. "If you remember, the Arts are somewhat of an iffy proposition in this world. I'm still working the bugs out of some new methods. Complicating things is the fact that the energy potential between the various universes has shifted over time. I'm still dealing with the implications of that."

"Ah, yes, I do seem to remember there was a very good reason why I didn't like New York and its provinces. No magic at all. Which made it an unacceptable alternative to Perilous, which fairly oozes with the damnable stuff."

"You never took to the Arts in a big way. Did you, Deems?"

"Never cared for hocus-pocus," Deems said with a shake of his head. "Never wanted any part of it. Makes me nervous."

"Although you need it occasionally."

"Occasionally," Deems conceded. "As do we all." He rubbed his belly and sighed.

"You've put on weight, elder brother."

Deems laughed. "Tell me something I don't know, little brother. I eat too much and drink even more. The Arts I'll have none of; the Vices, every one." He laughed heartily again, revealing large white teeth. When he was done he said, ''What are you up to, Inky?''

''Something's going on at Perilous, I don't quite know what. I suspect meddling. If that's the case, I haven't a clue as to who's the guilty party.''

''What sort of meddling?''

''A few of the spells sealing off some of the more troublesome aspects are completely gone. It could be that they deteriorated and simply fizzled out. It could also be that someone canceled them.''

''And you suspected . . . whom?''

''Trent, first off. One of the reasons I came here. I've been trying to detect evidence of major-magical activity in this universe. So far the data are inconclusive. If Trent is responsible, however, he may have taken great pains to cover his tracks.''

Deems nodded. ''And you suspect me?''

''Brother, you're at the bottom of the suspect list. Everyone knows you could have had the throne, but turned it down. Why then would you conspire now to take the throne from me?''

''I know of no reason,'' Deems said flatly.

''Nor do I.''

There was a pause before Deems asked, ''Then why this communication?''

''I wondered if you had any ideas. If you'd heard anything.''

''From who?''

''Ferne, for one. Have you seen her recently?''

''I haven't seen Ferne in a god's age.''

Incarnadine nodded. ''And Trent has never communicated with you in all this time?''

''I would have told you, just out of courtesy,'' Deems said.

''Just making sure, Deems. Trent says he wants to be left alone, and I have no reason yet not to take him at his word. But all the same, I have to be sure.''

''I can assure you that I am not in league with our little brother Trent.''

''I didn't say you were, Deems. In fact, I said I wanted your help.''

''I'll do anything I can.''

''Thank you. Ferne always liked Albion. Would you cast about and see if you can locate her there?''

''I'd be happy to, though I doubt she's here.''

''Nevertheless, if you find her, please tell her I wish to see her.''

"I will," Deems said. "Anything else?"

"Do you have enough Art to attempt calling Trent from your world?"

"No, I doubt it."

"Then, are you up for a short trip home?"

"Not exactly, but I will come if you insist."

"Then do, and be my guest. When you are here, use the Universal Projector to call him and sound him out. Tell me what you think. I need a second opinion, a second reading, if you will."

"Very well. I hope I can remember the spell that works that old contraption of Dad's. I haven't used it in years."

"Go to the library and look it up. Osmirik, the new librarian, will help you."

"It will be good to be back at Perilous again. I could use a change of scene." Deems scratched his black beard. "But won't Trent instantly suspect you put me up to it? I mean, calling him out of the blue, after so many years?"

"He may. I think he most probably will think I put you up to it. In fact, you can tell him I did. I want everything to be aboveboard, for now."

"As you wish. Do you suspect everyone? Dorcas as well?"

"Hardly Dorcas."

"Well, that more or less leaves Ferne, Trent, and me—and you say I'm out of the running."

"Ferne and Trent. Yes. They might be in it together. I find that not improbable. They always got along well together. In fact, Trent was the only one of us who was at all close to Ferne."

"It would seem a simple case, then, with only three possible solutions. It's either Ferne alone, or Trent alone, or both together."

"Or someone else entirely."

Deems scowled. "Who?"

"An outside force or agent of some sort."

Deems pursed his lips and looked pensive. "Hm. I suppose it's possible. Castle Perilous has never lacked for enemies."

"True."

"But see here. What's the game? What does this unknown conspirator mean to accomplish by opening up dangerous aspects and letting the boogeymen out?"

"The unknown may have struck some bargain with these boogeymen. They invade the castle in return for spoils he has promised."

"Which he can't deliver, unless he knows something I don't," Deems said sourly. "Out of 144,000 worlds, there isn't a single damn one that has any easy money in it. And I include the one you're in at the moment."

Incarnadine gave a chuckle. "Don't you remember all the time we spent panning for gold in Hyperborea, back when we were kids?"

"With not a penny to show for it."

"Now, I remember making enough to buy a very small sailboat," Incarnadine said. "A ten-foot sloop, as I recall. I think the thing may still be lying in a dusty corner of the castle somewhere. I used to take it out on Lake Asmodeus, in the Helvian aspect. I also have a memory of you buying yourself a silver-handled Almedian scimitar with the paydirt you gleaned."

Deems grunted. "I don't remember. It was a long time ago."

"Yes, it was."

"Tell me this, Inky. What could Trent have been doing, isolated in a blind universe all those years?" Deems' brow furrowed. "The thought occurs to me that *you* are now isolated in a blind universe. How the devil are you going to get back from there?"

"I'm going to do my damnedest to summon the gateway from this side and set up a more or less permanent link to Perilous. From a Manhattan apartment."

"Wasn't that where it was originally?"

"Yes. The site was not this specific apartment, but you remember the general location correctly. As to your first question about Trent—he says he hasn't, but I suspect he has been developing new magic on this side. He may have a way of summoning the gateway, using it, then letting it wander free again until he needs it. He may have had access to Castle Perilous all these years."

"Why has he waited all this time to make his move?"

"He may have been aiding Melydia. I rather doubt that, as Melydia was a major-league sorcerer herself, but she may have needed help at the interuniverse level."

"That is an interesting surmise."

"A wild guess. Perhaps Trent is patient. Or perhaps he's just recently perfected his techniques."

Deems folded his arms and looked dubious. "You really don't have much to go on, do you?"

"Frankly, no. That's why I was hoping you would help. When you return from Perilous, I want you to give me a rundown on what's happening there in my absence. Ask Tyrene, the captain of the Guard, to give you a report. Tell him I sent you.''

''If he believes me.'' Deems squinted one eye.

''He will. Before I left I told him to expect you.''

''I was going to ask why you can't call Tyrene yourself, but now I see you simply want to verify my trip to Perilous.'' Deems' eyes twinkled. ''You've been planning moves in advance.''

''As necessary in life as in chess.''

''Inky, I'll always defer to your chessmanship. How you outmaneuvered Melydia—that horror of a woman!—I'll never know.''

''Luck played its part—along with clean living, proper outlook, eating three squares a day, and so forth.''

Chuckling, Deems said, ''And regular exercise—no doubt.''

''When can you leave for Perilous?''

Deems shrugged. ''Today, if you wish. I have nothing pressing.''

''Good. Call me again, say, two days.''

''Very well. Anything else?''

''Not at the moment. Good seeing you again, brother.''

''Same here, old boy. But if you don't mind—'' Deems stood and reached out both arms toward the screen. The image jerked and the angle of view shifted until Deems' face was in close-up. ''I'm going to forgo the refined pleasures of having a mirror by the bed. I don't really care to be surprised in quite that way again. There are plenty of other looking-glasses about the palace.''

''My apologies.''

''So, if it's all the same to you—''

Deems carried the mirror through high mullioned doors and into open air. ''Goodbye, Incarnadine.'' Deems held the mirror out at arm's length, then let it drop.

The mirror turned slowly as it fell. The twisting perspective showed Deems standing on a balustrade high on the outside wall of the palace. He was looking down, smiling and waving. His image quickly shrank, sliding off to one side as the mirror turned to face the uprising ground. Briefly a tilted vista of the green and beautiful Albion countryside revealed itself until the screen of the CRT went black.

KEEP—QUEEN'S DINING HALL

SHEILA TOOK ANOTHER sip of coffee. She felt a little better now. There were people here who seemed to be in the same boat she was in—lost and stranded in a crazy place without knowing how or why. It felt good to talk to them and find out more about what the heck was going on here. None of what she was hearing made any sense, but at least everyone seemed to acknowledge that it *didn't* make any sense. She could deal with that. Not with everything not making sense, but with the fact that no one seemed concerned that it didn't.

Yes, she felt a little better, now that she had some proper clothes to wear. She had declined the usual quasi-medieval costume that everyone here pranced around in, opting instead for jeans, a blouse, and a good pair of running shoes. She'd been told that it was wise to be quick on your feet in Castle Perilous. She was determined to be as quick as possible.

The dining hall was almost full. Apparently it was a holiday in this world, and the castle servants (it was sometimes hard to tell the servants from the Guests, except that the servants had a sort of English accent) had set a festive table laden with dish after colorful and elaborate dish.

Everybody was digging in, so Sheila did, too.

"Anybody know what the occasion is?" Gene asked.

"Something akin to our winter solstice, I think," M. DuQuesne said.

"I guess most worlds have solstices and equinoxes and all that stuff," Gene said.

"My world doesn't," the creature called Snowclaw growled. (It seemed to growl all the time.) "Course, I wouldn't know what an eekinocks was if it came up and kicked me in the butt."

Sheila couldn't get over how she could understand everything the white-furred, white-clawed creature said. In fact, it sounded a little like Uncle Walt, Mom's brother. Uncle Walt growled a lot, too.

Despite her fear, she found the creature to be very friendly. She just couldn't bring herself to look into its fierce yellow eyes.

She helped herself to a slice of roast suckling pig, then spooned out samples of a few of the side dishes. Everything had been delicious so far.

"Snowclaw, your world has to have an equinox," Gene insisted.

"How do you know?" Snowclaw scoffed. "You've never been there."

"Does it have a sun?"

"Well, of course."

"Then it has equinoxes and solstices. What I'm talking about is . . . well, really it's the relationship of a sun to a planet that revolves about it. You see, when a planet's axis of rotation is tilted somewhat to the plane of its orbit, what happens is that—"

"What's a planet?"

"Uh, a planet. It's a world. You know, a big spherical lump of dirt that spins around."

"Spins around what?"

"Turns. Rotates."

"Where?"

Gene blinked. "What do you mean, 'Where'? Out in space, of course. Look, when a planet spins on its axis, it—"

"What's space?"

Gene took a long drink from his beer stein. "Forget it."

"Anything you say, pal," Snowclaw said amiably.

M. DuQuesne said, "Snowclaw, does your world have a warm season and a cold season?"

"Sure does."

"Is the sun a little lower in the sky in the cold season?"

"It's a lot lower."

"Then, when the sun is at its lowest point during the cold season, and the days are very short, that's the winter solstice. When it's at its highest point in the sky during the warm season, and the days are long, that's the summer solstice. The equinoxes are in between, in spring and autumn, when night and day are about equally long.''

"Oh. Well, sure, everybody knows that! Thanks.''

Everyone looked at Gene. He shrugged. "Okay, so I'm not Isaac Asimov.''

A man called Thaxton said, "Who's for tennis today?''

Another, older man who called himself Cleve Dalton said, "Thax old boy, you ask that every damn day, and I can't recall that anyone's ever taken you up on it. Where the devil are the courts, anyway?''

"Well, they're through an aspect just a little down the hall to the right. I suspect they're not really tennis courts per se. I mean, there are nets and such, but they actually seem to be—''

There came shouts from out in the hallway, and the sound of running feet. A man, one of the servants, came running through the main entrance looking frightened to death. He ran past the table and shouted, "They're coming! Run for your lives!'' He sprinted to the kitchen entrance, threw the door open, and dashed through.

Everyone froze for a moment. Then Gene said, "It's gotta be the Bluefaces.''

As if to corroborate his remark, three Bluefaces stormed through the main entrance with drawn swords.

"Stay where you are!'' the middle one commanded. "You are now under authority of His Imperial Domination, High Proconsul of Greater Borjakshann, and you are subject to his every whim, wish, and caprice!''

"Hey, Blueface!''

Somewhat nonplussed, the creature raked an eye up and down the table until it found the speaker.

"Who dares defy authority of Proconsul?''

Snowclaw rose to his full height. "Me, that's who,'' he said.

The creature looked a trifle uncertain. "Any resistance will be dealt with harshly!''

"Yeah? What are you gonna do, bleed on me?''

The Blueface grinned with a satisfied malevolence. "For that bit of insolence, you will be put to death immediately!''

With a blood-congealing howl, Snowclaw sprang into a blur of motion. In one clean jump from a standstill, he was up on the table and running, huge clawed feet picking their way through the soup tureens and serving plates of prime rib, executing a neat end run around the carved ice centerpiece. At some point he became airborne, taloned toes leading, the claws of his hands swiping at the air, mouth wide and bristling with wickedly sharp teeth, gleaming incisors almost big enough to be tusks. A fire of diabolical ferocity burned in his alien yellow eyes.

The Blueface barely had time to point its sword in the proper direction. To no avail. The splayed foot of Snowclaw's long right leg, which had extended slightly, hit the invader squarely in the breastplate. The sword went flying, and the creature went down, Snowclaw crashing on top of it.

Gene had delayed only an instant. He was up and charging by the time Snowclaw had made his leap.

"Everybody out through the kitchen!" he yelled.

Four more blue-skinned soldiers stormed through the door, and a few of the other males and one woman jumped up and ran to meet them, swords drawn.

Sheila just sat there, a morsel of beef Stroganoff still poised on the end of her fork, her mouth hanging open.

Ohmygawd. What the *hell* is happening now?

Someone grabbed her arm. It was Linda Barclay.

"Sheila! Run!"

Sheila got up and joined the clot of people that had jammed up at the kitchen door. She looked back over her shoulder to see Gene Ferraro crossing swords with one of the creatures, while the big white beast karate-fought with another. The Blueface who had done all the talking was sprawled on the floor with purple gunk running out of its mouth. Sheila suddenly got very sick, and very afraid.

Gene swung his weapon and lopped off the sword-arm of his opponent. Sheila saw the severed blue member splat to the floor. She thought she would throw up then and there, but when Gene's next stroke clove the creature's skull in two, spraying purple liquid all over the place, she was too shocked to react. Meanwhile, Snowclaw had lifted his adversary over his head; he threw the creature against the stone wall. The Blueface hit with a bone-pulping thud, hung against the wall for an impossible instant, then clattered to the floor.

Gene ran for the door. "Come on, Snowy, there's too many of them!"

Snowclaw batted at one of the new intruders and sent the creature flying, but when he saw more reinforcements streaming through the main entrance, he broke for the back door.

Sheila had been watching all this, half hypnotized by the savagery of it, half paralyzed with fear. Linda yanked her back through the door as Gene came charging through.

Linda, Sheila, Gene, and Snowclaw raced through the cluttered, now deserted kitchen and banged out through the opposite door. They were followed by three survivors of the group who had joined the fight. The woman was not with them.

Once outside the kitchen, they pushed a huge sideboard against the door to block it. Immediately grunts and crashing sounds issued from the other side.

"They killed Morgana," one of the men told Gene. "She chopped up one of them before getting it from behind."

"I saw," Gene said. "We'd better split up."

The other nodded. "My favorite aspect is down this way."

"Maybe not such a good idea," Gene said. "Better to get off into the remote parts of the castle. Of course, that's just a guess. You make your own decision."

"Good luck."

"Same to you." Gene turned to Linda. "You and Sheila coming with us?"

"Of course. Gene, you were marvelous. I can't believe how good a swordfighter you are. Maybe you really are Cyrano de Bergerac."

"No, I just have a nose for trouble."

Sheila hoped he was Cyrano, Duke Wayne, and Sylvester Stallone all rolled into one.

164 EAST 64TH STREET

HE SAT HUNCHED over, his forehead in one palm, elbow on the desk, peering down at a sheet of paper that crawled with arcane mathematical symbols. A high pile of crumpled sheets lay to his right. Stacks of books lay about the desk, interspersed with pencils and other writing implements, three or four different types of electronic calculator, several empty aluminum soda cans, and a cup and saucer holding the dregs of two-day-old coffee.

He threw down his pencil, a weary scowl on his face. "Dung of a thousand kine!"

There was not much enthusiasm in the curse. "Shit," he added, with not much more.

He exhaled and peered into the coffee cup. He *yecched* silently, got up, and carried it into the kitchen, where he set about inducing Mr. Coffee to do its job. He spooned grounds into a fresh paper filter and slid the little drawer holding the filter into the machine, then poured cold water into the top of the device.

In the living room, the computer beeped a warning. He rushed directly to it and sat at the terminal.

He typed, NATURE OF EMERGENCY?

The disk drive rumbled. Then the screen displayed: *DANGER.*

RANGE AND DIRECTION? he queried.

NEARBY AND CLOSING FROM WEST.

GROUND OR AIRBORNE?
GROUND.
NATURE OR EMBODIMENT OF DANGER?
UNABLE TO DETERMINE.

''That's a fine how-do-you-do,'' he muttered. CAN PINPOINT PROXIMITY?

NEAR was all it answered.

''Damn program is full of bugs! Full of them!''

He halted waving his arms and considered his outburst. ''I'm losing it. I'll have to pull myself together.''

His eyes closed and his shoulders relaxed. He remained motionless for several minutes.

Presently the intercom buzzed. He opened his eyes, took a deep breath, and got up.

''Yes?''

''Mr. Carney?'' It was the doorman.

''Yes.''

''Express package for you. Should I send the guy up?''

''Just take delivery. I'll be down for it later.''

''He says you gotta sign for it.''

He considered the matter. The package would doubtless be the books he had ordered from a small specialty bookstore in San Francisco, whose owner had promised to get them out on the next plane yesterday afternoon. He was not yet acquainted enough with the minutiae of this world to judge the degree of risk.

But he really had to know, didn't he?

''Have him come up.''

He sat down and closed his eyes again, preparing himself, until the door chimed.

The express man was young and looked innocuous enough.

''Hi! Mr. John Carney?''

''You got 'im.''

The express man shoved the package toward him. It was heavy and he had to use both hands to accept it. Heavy enough to be books.

''Just sign here, sir,'' the man said, proffering a clipboard and pen.

''Just a minute.''

He turned, walked into the apartment, and laid the package on the dinette table. As he did, he heard the door close behind him. The computer began to beep frantically.

He whirled in time to see the delivery man drawing a large-caliber, silencer-tipped revolver. He dropped behind the dinette table just as the hit man fired, the bullet thunking into the package. He crawled behind an easy chair, then leaped out, diving toward the door of the darkened bedroom. The next two shots chipped wood from the doorframe above his head as he sailed through.

He crawled to the far end of the bed and remained on the floor.

Then, reaching into a place that was not exactly a place, which lay in a direction that was not quite up or down or to or fro, he summoned the thing that he found there, and it came forth. From what time or space or continuum the thing had come, he neither knew nor cared.

It stood above him, a mass of gleaming metal trimmed with strips of black synthetic material. Its arms ended in huge steel claws, and its head was a clear bubble housing whirling sensors and flashing probes. Thin, many-colored lines of light danced in crosshatch patterns on the walls of the dim bedroom, shifting and changing as the device took readings and measurements. In less than a second it was ready to move.

It clanked around the bed and rolled through the doorway into the hall.

There came a yelp, then another muffled gunshot and the spang of a bullet ricocheting off metal.

"DESTROY," the mechanical thing stated, raising its arms. The claws swung to one side and dangerous-looking rods protruded from the cavities within the arms.

"No!" he shouted from the bedroom.

"I'm leaving!" the express man shouted.

There came the sounds of hasty retreat. Then the front door slammed.

"NOT DESTROY?" was the query with a slight note of disappointment.

"No. Scan premises for enemy."

"SECTOR CLEAR."

He came out from the bedroom. The machine was already fading.

"WILL NOT BE REDEPLOYED?" the thing asked.

"Return to post," he ordered, which it was doing, anyway.

It was gone in the next instant.

He locked the door, slid the dead bolt, and affixed the chain. He retrieved the package. The books he had ordered were in it, one with a deformed slug inside that had bored clear through to page 457, which began a chapter titled "Incantations Useful in Interdimensional Quantum Transformations."

He went into the kitchen and poured himself a cup of fresh-brewed coffee.

LIBRARY

OSMIRIK CARRIED THE heavy folio up the stairs to his favorite carrel, which was tucked into a vault on the first gallery. He liked the spot, snugly surrounded as it was by his favorite things, namely books; but now it would afford him safe haven in more than a spiritual sense. That is, it would if all his hastily made plans worked out. He meant to take advantage of one of the castle's architectural peculiarities. If all else failed, an exit lay close by, should the need for such arise.

Arise it doubtless would, and soon. The invaders would hardly overlook the castle's library, surely the largest depository of learning in this world. If they coveted the castle's secrets, only its library could provide the key.

What Osmirik sought was the key to fight the invaders, and that could only be found in certain ancient texts contained in this library and this library alone. This huge folio was one such text, a work written by Ervoldt, the ancient Haplodite King who had "built" Castle Perilous—or, to be more accurate, had caused it to be created, some three millennia ago.

He sidled into the narrow carrel. Sighing, he sat down and opened the leather-bound volume, which in gilt lettering bore the simple title *Ervoldt, His Book*. The language and script in which the work had been written was called Haplan, which he had diligently studied since beginning his tenure as chief librarian at Castle Perilous, almost a year ago to the day. (The post had been vacant for fifty years before he took it up.)

He turned to the first page, and his former wonder was renewed. This was no codex, no painstakingly handwritten work of a copyist. This was a printed text, which would not be surprising were it not for the fact that it was over three thousand years old. The beautiful vellum paper was not even yellowed. Printing had not existed three thousand years ago, nor three hundred—except, obviously, in Castle Perilous, by whose magic all manner of things was possible.

The author's prefatory material was short. In fact, it was rather blunt:

> Ye who scan this Book be well advised; that its Scribe be no Man of Poesy, nor Aesthete given to Niceties of Phrase. For Such and their Ilk I care not Pig Leavings. I set down the Words as they come, as they are needed for their appointed Tasks, and as I see fit; no more or less do I set down. For I, Ervoldt, King by the Grace of the Gods, have a Story, and I will let nothing bar the way of its Telling. I will leave out nothing of Substance. Neither will I embellish. What is ugly, I will render ugly; what is beautiful needs little by my Hand. I will tell what I must, and no more, and when the Telling is done, I will be done. If any find Fault with this, or me, I say read another Book, and be damned.

Somewhat brusque, but to the point, and possessing a certain admirable muscularity of phrase. But Osmirik had no time for literary criticism. His task was to glean practical knowledge from this work, not to judge its author's prose style. Moreover—

There came a loud crashing from below. Osmirik jumped up, left the vault, and went to the rail of the gallery. Below, the huge main room was as deserted as before—nothing but row upon row of open stacks with a few tables interspersed—but now he could identify the source of the noise. Someone was trying to break through the massive oak of the front doors, which were bolted and barred from the inside. Very likely the invaders were on the other side.

Another crash, and Osmirik saw the doors shake. He dashed back to his nook and drew out the parcel that he had laid inside. It was crammed with victuals, enough to last him days. A chamber pot lay underneath the table, along with a supply of candles and some blankets.

He stood and ran his hand along the back of the stone ribbing that formed the inside arch of the doorway. Finding a small block of wood there, he pressed it. There came the rumble of sliding stone. He stepped back as a massive stone barrier slid across to seal the vault off like a tomb. Osmirik exhaled and listened to the silence. This small chamber was one of hundreds used to store rare volumes of inestimable worth. It also made an excellent redoubt for a librarian.

The vault was completely dark. Cursing himself for not doing it before, he sought candle and flint wheel. At length he managed to get a flame from the wheel, lit a candle, and stood it in its sconce on the table. The tiny chamber filled with yellow light. The flame of the candle guttered. The place was well ventilated. He would be fine here, for a while. He had light, air, food, and books—and he could catch a few winks under the table. No one could find him, no one would bother him, not even the Hell-begotten blue demons.

Now, all he had to do was discover what particular hell had begotten them.

KEEP

GENE STEPPED OVER the body of another castle Guardsman. He had lost track of how many they had encountered.

"The Bluefaces are everywhere," he said to Linda. "It's a well-organized and coordinated attack. Meticulously planned, too, I'll bet."

"What should we do?" Linda asked.

"Leave the castle. Have any preferences as to what aspect we dive through?"

"Oh, any nice place with trees and grass, I guess."

"Trees and grass? How about a source of food? Remember, when you leave the castle, your magic stays here. No more whipping up quick meals with a wave of the hand."

"That's going to be somewhat of a problem."

They continued down the hallway cautiously, Gene in the lead and Snowclaw bringing up the rear. Sheila tagged close to Linda, whose hand she occasionally sought when danger neared. Linda didn't look as scared as Sheila was. But then, Linda was used to this place. Sheila didn't understand how anyone could get used to a nightmare, but she was more than willing to stick close to anyone who could.

They walked on a little farther until they came to a crossing corridor, at which they stopped. Gene poked his head around the corner.

"It's clear." As he took a step forward, grunting sounds came from far down the hall to the left. Gene backstepped hastily, bumping into Linda. "Company coming!" he whispered.

They backtracked to an empty alcove and crowded into it. Sheila squeezed in next to Snowclaw, noticing how smooth and silky his fur was.

The rumble of heavy running feet sounded. Gene knelt, peered around the corner, and saw Bluefaces streaming through the intersection of the corridors.

"There must be thirty of 'em. No, fifty."

The thunder of footsteps receded, diminishing to distant echoes.

Gene took a breath. "They must have invaded with a force in the thousands. They've probably already taken over key points in the castle."

"We don't have much of a chance," Linda said.

"Not unless we find an acceptable gateway soon. If this keeps up, we might have to take the next one we run across."

"I'd invite you all to my world," Snowclaw said, "except that it's pretty darn cold there, and you hairless types might not take to it. Besides, the portal's on the other side of the castle."

"I'd put up with the cold," Gene said. "The more unattractive the world, the less chance the Bluefaces might be interested in it."

"Maybe so," Snowclaw said. "Well, you're all welcome to stay in my shack for as long as you like. I wouldn't mind the company." He scratched his belly absently. "We'd be a little crowded, though."

Gene said, "Snowy, I've always wanted to see your world, but I'm going to keep it as a last resort." Gene leaned against the wall and scratched under his cuirass. "Damn it, all the best portals are in the Guest areas, which is where most of the invaders are going to be hanging out, of course."

"The one with the golf course is nice," Linda said. "And the little dinosaur-humanoids are friendly."

"Primitive," Gene said, shaking his head. "Hot, and dangerous. Outside the little resort area, it's pretty rough out there in the jungle. And the Bluefaces will be all through there, I bet."

"And we saw them on the picnic world," Linda said. "So much for that."

"We must have looked into hundreds of portals since we've been here. There are 144,000 of them in the castle. Try to think of one that we can hide out in for a while."

"Well, there's the one with the forest and the waterfall."

"Same problem, it's near the Guest area."

"Right," Linda said. "I've always liked the one that sort of looks like a Japanese garden."

"Ditto."

"Oh, you're right. Well, how about—?" Linda was stumped.

"Now, there was one with a little village nearby with nice sorts of native people. Little pale people with big golden eyes. They'd gladly put us up for a spell, I think. Damned if I can remember where the hell the portal was, though."

"I remember!" Linda said.

"Shhhh! Keep your voice down."

"Sorry. I was just thinking of one. It's not too far from here, if I recall. It's near the castle armory, and—" Her face fell. "Oh, dear."

"The armory's probably the first objective the Bluefaces took, along with the Guard garrison. You have to remember—"

Sounds of approaching footsteps came from the direction in which the Blueface troop had marched.

"They're coming back," Gene said. "Come on!"

They ran. At the next intersecting hallway, they took the right branch, running a spell until they came to a stairwell. This they descended one level, where they found quiet.

"Hell," Gene complained. "Look, we need to think, and plan. Let's get to someplace where we can do it, like Snowy's world. There, at least, we won't be bothered, and we can come up with some answers."

"Will we be able to get back into the castle?" Linda said.

Gene thoughtfully rubbed the stubble on his chin. "Good point. The castle's a big place, but maybe they have enough troops to block every portal. No telling."

"So, what do we do?"

Gene shrugged. "Keep moving until we find a good aspect, jump in, and hope the Bluefaces won't follow us."

"Back to square one," Linda said. She thought awhile, then said, "How about we hide out in the wilder parts of the castle?"

Gene looked dubious.

Sheila asked, "What do you mean, Linda?"

Linda squatted and leaned against a pillar. "Well, some parts of the castle are stable, like the Guest areas. You know, like where the dining hall is? Around there. But other parts of the castle aren't so stable."

"In fact," Gene said, "they're absolutely crazy."

Sheila nodded. Crazy. If what she'd already seen of the place was *sane* . . . Ohmygawd.

"And dangerous," Gene added. "But on second thought, not quite as dangerous, maybe, as what we're facing here."

"Maybe not," Linda agreed. "I think it might be worth the risk."

"Isn't there some way of . . . you know, *leaving* the castle?" Sheila asked. "Just going outside, the regular way?"

"There's not much out there," Gene said. "We've been told that most of the people who live in these parts stay in the castle. I don't blame them. It's pretty bleak."

"Oh." Sheila slumped against the cold stone of the wall.

Grunting voices came from the right.

"Let's move," Gene said calmly.

They ran from the voices, but made it only a short way down the corridor before hearing echoing footsteps ahead. They took the left branch of the nearest intersection, sprinted to the next crossing, stopped, and looked both ways before going on.

Voices behind them, now voices in front again. They backtracked and went left, ran and then dashed right, only to hear the flapping steps of flat, webbed feet everywhere they turned.

"It's no use," Gene said, stopping for breath. "Linda, you gotta use your magic. We have to go either up or down in a hurry."

"Stairs?"

"No, something faster!"

"What? I can't think of anything that wouldn't be mechanical, like an elevator or something."

Grunting sounds came from the left, then, after a moment, from behind.

"Think!" Gene whispered hoarsely.

Linda closed her eyes. A soft popping sound came from behind Gene, and he turned to look. A neatly cut hole had appeared in the stone floor. A shiny brass pipe, about three inches in diameter, ran from the ceiling down through the hole.

"A firehouse pole?" Gene shrugged. "Hey, why not? Let's go, gang."

Gene was first. He slid out of sight quickly, and Linda followed.

"Let's go, little girl," Snowclaw urged gently.

Sheila leaned out, grabbed the pole, and jumped, locking her legs around the slippery brass shaft. The drop was heart-stoppingly fast, and only frantic contractions of her leg muscles finally slowed her. Despite her best efforts, she landed hard on her buttocks.

Gene dragged her up. "Again," he ordered Linda.

"Again?"

"Down another floor. Can't you hear them up there?"

Linda whipped up another pole as Snowclaw dropped down and corroborated, "They're coming!"

They all slipped down the new fire pole. This time Sheila was determined to land on her feet, and she did.

"Again," Gene said.

They dropped four levels in all before Gene realized it was useless.

"They're simply following us down," he said. "We're just not thinking, gang."

Linda said, "Then we're sunk. I can't make things disappear." She blinked, then smiled. "But I can make a ladder!"

The hole appeared, as before, but this time a wooden ladder angled up from it. They clambered down one by one. On the lower level, Gene and Snowclaw slid the bottom of the ladder across the flagstone until the upper end slipped out of the hole above. The ladder clattered to the floor.

They repeated this procedure three more times before coming to a quiet level.

Gene looked up. "Linda, I want you to conjure a sort of thing that looks like a drain stopper, but made out of heavy stone, one just big enough to plug that hole up there."

"A drain stopper?"

"Imagine a big heavy thing like a stone mushroom, with the stem plugging the hole."

"Got you."

The bottom of the plug fit neatly flush with the ceiling.

"Good job. I don't think they'll be able to lift that thing very easily."

"Great idea, Gene," Linda said.

"Should have come up with it sooner. But when you're on the run, it's hard to be creative."

"Man, you gotta think fast in this place!" Sheila said breathlessly.

"Even more so, down here," Gene told her. "Stay close, and watch your step."

"What's down here?"

"Expect the unexpected."

"Like . . . what, exactly?"

Bright daylight flooded the corridor. Sheila whirled and beheld what looked at first like a movie screen, except that the images were three-dimensional. Then her mind made the connection that this was some sort of opening that had suddenly appeared. Through the rectangular portal lay a short expanse of white beach, leading to foaming breakers. The surf was close, very close. In fact . . .

"You better get back, Sheila," Gene said.

She watched, transfixed, as a swell rose up, rode in, and broke very near the opening. Sheila squealed and backstepped as the surf foamed through the portal and across the floor, slopping over her shoes.

She squished down the corridor to where the others had sought dry floor. They were smiling at her.

"I see what you mean," Sheila said.

"Is that your first wild aspect?" Gene asked. "Strange, isn't it? The aspects you see through the windows aren't so startling. You look out and see weird things, but somehow, the window comfortably frames it. But when you see an aspect pop out of nowhere like that—"

"It kind of blows your mind," Sheila said, nodding gravely. "Why are they called aspects?"

"Just a term that's used around here. They're called aspects, portals, gateways . . . other things."

Suddenly the sunlight faded, and the sound of breakers stopped abruptly. They all turned to find that the portal had vanished.

"There it goes," Gene said, "just as mysteriously as it appeared."

Sheila shook her head slowly. "Where *was* that place? That ocean?"

"It could have been the beach at Malibu," Gene told her. "Or somewhere on the Gold Coast of Africa. But I looked, and I didn't see anything out there that would lead me to believe it was a way back to Earth. It could have been any one of tens of thousands of worlds. Probably a deserted planet, somewhere, in an uninhabited star system a billion light-years from—'' He shrugged. ''Wherever.''

''Was the one I fell through like that?'' Sheila asked.

''Probably. Just like the ones we blundered through.''

Sheila stared off into the darkness. ''Maybe it actually was a way back. Back home.''

''We'll never know, Sheila. Best not to think about it. We're stranded here, in this world, this castle. You'd better start getting used to the notion of being here for a while.''

Sheila grunted ironically. ''A while? You mean for the rest of my life.'' Brow knitted, she massaged her bottom lip between her teeth. Then, murmuring to herself: ''But I really didn't have much of a life, did I?''

Gene said, ''I'm sorry. What did you say?''

Sheila took a deep breath and turned around. ''Nothing. Nothing at all.''

Gene smiled at her. ''Don't worry. In time, you'll actually get to like it here. I look at it as sort of an extended vacation. Two weeks in August that never seem to end. But at some point it will, it must. A gateway will pop up in front of us, leading right into Times Square, and the vacation will be over. It'll be September, time to go back to school. Or to a new job.''

Sheila studied him clinically. He wasn't a bad-looking fellow, rather tall, with curly dark brown hair and gray-green eyes. Not bad over all, except that she would never have given him a second look on the street, or in a bar. He had a boyish, immature way about him, even though he talked very well and sounded educated. She liked him. ''You really believe we'll get back someday, don't you?''

Something deep in his eyes flashed when he smiled. ''You bet. This is a dream—a shared dream. And someday we'll all wake up.''

She managed to smile back at him, and it made her feel good. ''Anyone for lunch?''

Gene and Sheila looked. Linda had conjured an impressive buffet table laden with an endless assortment of cold cuts and salads.

''Come and get it before it goes up in a puff of smoke,'' Linda said.

Snowclaw swiped at a plate and came away with about three

pounds of sliced roast beef. He shoved the mass into his mouth, chewed four times—no more—and swallowed. He shook his head wearily. "You know, I keep trying this stuff you guys like. It's good, don't get me wrong. But a little while later and I'm hungry again."

"Try a little mustard with it," Linda suggested, tossing him a jar of Dijon. Unbelieving, she watched Snowclaw pop it into his mouth. "Snowy, don't!"

The glass crunched horribly. "Hey, now you're talking!" Snowclaw said with a satisfied grin.

KEEP—LOWER LEVELS

BARNABY WALSH WAS exhausted. He was by nature a sedentary person, tending to avoid movement unless dire necessity demanded it, and this frantic chasing about, keeping one step ahead of the Bluefaces, was more than his ill-proportioned, overweight body could stand. In fact, he simply couldn't take another step. . . .

"We can't stop!" Deena Williams yelled at him.

"I gotta," Barnaby told her, slumping against the wall.

Deena ran back and yanked at a handful of his shirt. "Come on, man! They're right behind us!"

"I can't . . . run . . . anymore," Barnaby wheezed at her. "I'm completely . . . I can't—"

"You gotta! The Bluefaces are comin'!"

"But . . ." Barnaby tried to swallow the acrid dryness at the back of his throat. He choked and coughed, bending over double.

"Shhhh!" Deena looked worriedly back down the passageway. "Keep it quiet, or they gonna get us."

Barnaby recovered enough to say, "I can't go on. I'm done."

"No, you're not. Just keep puttin' one foot in front of the other. Come on, man, you can do it."

"No, honest."

He looked at her. She wasn't even breathing hard! But she'd

been a track athlete in high school, she'd said, before getting pregnant and dropping out. She had always dreamed of going to the Olympics. She was even dressed for the part, in a purple sweatshirt, red shorts, and white running shoes.

"Go ahead," he told her. "Take off. I'll just hold you up."

Scowling, she shook him hard. "Don't start that hero stuff with me, you hear? I'll slap you silly. Now, let's go, unless you wanna mess with them blue dudes."

"Okay, okay," Barnaby groaned. Grunting noises from behind gave him the added impetus to start moving again. He staggered forward, steadied himself with one hand on the wall, then boosted his pace to a painful, galumphing jog, his oversize wing-tip oxfords slapping against the flagstone.

They ran. The place was nothing but endless corridors shunting every which way, leading to nothing but more passageways and corridors and the occasional crypt or alcove, all of it giving the impression of having been laid out without design, purpose, or plan.

I'm no hero, Barnaby thought to himself. In fact, he was just the opposite. He was more afraid now than he had ever been at any time in his life. He had told her to go on without him as a sort of test. He didn't know what he would have done had she left. Alone, he might have simply gone insane.

They made their way down the stone-walled corridor, Deena at a sprint, Barnaby loping along. She reached a cross-tunnel and stopped until he caught up.

"Stairs," she said, pointing to the left.

Barnaby could barely see in the gloom. "Let's go," he said.

The stairwell was spiral. Deena started down the well, taking two steps at a time, her crisp white athletic shoes glowing in the darkness.

Barnaby said, "I can barely—" then stumbled and almost fell.

Deena halted a few turns down. "Watch yourself," she warned. "It's dark down here."

"Yeah," he said dully.

They continued down, and found to their dismay that the stairwell was endless. After five minutes of steady descent they stopped, not knowing what to do.

"Go back up?" Deena suggested.

Barnaby gave her an incredulous look.

"Guess not." She shrugged. "They gotta end sometime."

They kept on following the downward spiral for another ten minutes. The stairwell continued with no sign of a bottom.

"Shit!"

"It's ridiculous," Barnaby said.

"Silliest damn thing," Deena complained, hands on her hips and a look of offended dignity on her dark brown face. She sneered up, then down. "Damn. Well, if we didn't go back up before, we sure ain't gonna do it now. Let's go."

They stumped down the stairs for another five or ten minutes. The stairwell was bare and featureless, except for an occasional glowing jewel-torch and the odd niche here and there.

"I'm really starting to get pissed off," Deena said.

Barnaby couldn't help laughing. Deena caught it and began to giggle. She continued doing so, intermittently, for the next few minutes, but as time wore on, she fell silent save for occasional grumbling and cursing.

They marched down the spiral for a quarter hour before the stairs eventually ended in a low-ceilinged tunnel.

"Finally," Barnaby murmured, barely able to keep his legs moving. He was beyond fatigue now; he wondered how long his heart would last, how long it would keep feebly pushing blood through his bloated carcass, which now felt like something dead that had to be dragged along.

The tunnel went straight for a stretch, then made a forty-five-degree turn, followed by a right-angled corner. The passage continued for about sixty feet, ultimately feeding into another stairwell whose spiraling steps led nowhere but up.

"Oh, no!" Barnaby staggered backward.

"Damn," she said. "They *screwin'* with us!"

"Oh my God." Barnaby collapsed against the cold stone wall of the tunnel. He sank to his haunches and closed his eyes.

Deena sat on the steps and began tenderly massaging her firm, almost muscular brown legs. "They jerkin' us around."

Barnaby didn't speak; he couldn't. They sat in silence for a long spell.

"Damn," she said again, quietly. And then, after a long pause: "Well . . ."

"Don't even think of it," Barnaby said.

"Okay," she said. "Take your time. We ain't exactly got anywhere to go."

"Thanks."

"But up."

"Exactly."

She craned her neck, peering up the spiral. "Maybe it don't go up as far as the other one went down."

"Why can't I believe that?" Barnaby said.

"'Cause they *screwin'* with us, that's why," Deena said. Then she began giggling again.

Barnaby answered with a hideous laugh, which made Deena giggle all the more. Barnaby closed his eyes again and laughed till it hurt.

He choked it off when Deena suddenly yelped and jumped up from the steps as if from a hot stove.

"What the hell—?" She stared in disbelief at the steps, which, inexplicably, had begun moving upward of their own accord, like some impossible stone escalator.

Getting to his feet, Barnaby acted as though he wasn't at all surprised. He caught the bottom step, mounted, and rose up the stairwell.

"Going up—lingerie, notions, merchandise return on the mezzanine."

"I'm comin'," Deena told him, stepping aboard. "I just wish this *was* Bloomingdale's," she added in a mutter.

They rose in silence, the paradoxical escalator making a barely audible humming noise. Gradually its speed increased, and the stairwell showed no sign of ending. Eyes wide with wonder, Barnaby and Deena continued their magical ascent. Air whistled past them down the spiraling shaft. The rate of climb kept steadily increasing. In a few minutes it began to take on alarming proportions.

"What was that you said about the mezzanine?" she asked nervously. "I want to get off."

"Yeah," he said, licking dry lips. "This seemed a peachy idea down at the bottom."

The noise increased to a thunderous roar, and the escalator's speed soon necessitated their getting down on all fours to fight a centrifugal force that threatened to push them into the stationary outside wall, which was rushing by at a rate guaranteed to impart a severe brush burn at the very least. But there was nothing to hold on to but bare stone.

It was like being inside a tumble-dryer. Soon, the walls became a blur and vertigo overtook both of them. Barnaby felt consciousness slipping away as his hands inexorably slid across the smooth stone of the steps. . . .

He reached the brink of oblivion, then came back, and he realized that the escalator was slowing down. He held on tightly until it came to an abrupt stop.

They lay motionless for a moment. Barnaby raised his head. There was a landing a few steps up. He slowly got to his feet, then looked back at Deena, who was rising. He held out his hand, and she took it.

"Come on," he said.

They mounted the last few steps and came out into an expansive room with numerous windowed alcoves. Daylight streamed through some of the windows. There were a few tables and chairs lying about, and one leather-covered settee, which Barnaby collapsed across, stretching out facedown. Deena sat down on the backs of his legs, and, fashioned like this, they rested for a full ten minutes.

Eventually he said, "My legs are falling asleep."

"Sorry, I couldn't get up."

"It's okay."

Deena rose and moved to a chair. Barnaby levered himself upright. "Jesus," he sighed.

"Yeah, ain't it the truth."

Presently Deena got up and wandered over to one of the alcoves.

"What the *hell* is this shit?" she wanted to know.

"What?" he asked, still too tired to move.

"You gotta see this."

"In a minute . . . or two, or three."

"Barnaby, you gotta see this crazy shit! This is insane!"

"Oh. Well, for the merely crazy, I wouldn't stir myself. But for the truly irrational . . ." He cranked himself off the settee, went over to the alcove, and stood next to her, looking out the open window.

Outside the window, there was no castle. The window itself was simply a rectangular hole in the middle of the air, suspended about five feet above an arid plain. In the distance lay a gigantic egg-shaped crystal bubble covering the polyhedral buildings and tall towers of a wildly futuristic city. Something about it made it look deserted. A slow wind moved across the plain; all was silent.

"Jesus," Barnaby said.

"Where the hell is that place?"

Barnaby shook his head slowly. "Who knows? Somewhere in time and space."

Deena snorted contemptuously. "Time and space, huh? I think it's *crazy*."

"They told me about these floating aspects. They're a little less stable than the kind you can just walk through. But they generally stay put."

"I never seen one like this. Most of 'em have different scenery and stuff, but I ain't never seen one with a space city in it."

"You think it's somewhere out in space?" he asked in wonderment. "On another planet?"

"Damn' if I know. Sure looks like it."

"I wonder . . ." He swallowed and massaged his throat with a thumb and forefinger. "I wonder who—or what—lives in that city."

"I don't know, and I don't wanna know. Let's look through the other windows. It's gonna be more crazy shit, I bet."

It was. The window to the right looked out onto a vast desert of wind-furrowed sand, and the next one down was a breathtaking view of an alpine meadow, snow-capped peaks in the distance. The next was dark—there was nothing out there but the distant cries in the night. The fifth window looked out on brackish marshes, and the next presented the green and pleasant aspect of a park.

"This is pretty nice," she said. "Let's take a walk."

He gulped. "Out . . . there?"

"Yeah, why not? Better than this crummy place." Deena stuck her head out, looking down. "It's only two foot off the ground. We can jump it easy. Come on." She swung one meaty leg up over the stone windowsill.

Barnaby was hesitant. "Do you really think we should?"

Deena brought her other leg up, sat momentarily, then jumped off. She landed lightly, bouncing up and down a few times to test the footing. "It's okay," she said. "Come on."

Barnaby climbed through the window and jumped down, falling to his knees in soft shoe-high grass. He got up. They were in a wide clearing; the surrounding woods were thick, but almost no underbrush grew between the tall, slender trees. The sky was soft blue, shading to yellowish white toward a bright sun directly overhead. The air was warm, and there was the smell of green and growing things in the air.

"Nice," Deena said.

"Yeah," he agreed.

They wandered together for a few paces, then went off separately, she to examine a bed of wildflowers, he to find a place to take a leak. He didn't want to go off very far, but the only cover nearby lay among a grove of tall bushes at the edge of the clearing. He wished something better were available, but duty called, so he struck off for the woods.

Glancing about nervously, he relieved himself. It was one of those extended sessions, long delayed, that never seem to stop. Finally it did, and he was zipping himself up when he heard Deena yell for him. He dashed out from the bushes.

The clearing was full of animals that looked somewhat like lions, were it not for the elaborate coral-colored, antlerlike organs that blossomed from their shaggy heads. Their coloring was tawny, lionlike, but their legs and bodies were longer and thinner, and they had no tails. There were about eight of them, and one was advancing toward him, growling with saber-teeth bared.

Deena was standing near the spot where the floating window had been, but there was no chance of her escaping. The aperture now hung a good ten feet off the ground. Apparently it had drifted.

Four of the creatures had her encircled, and several more were stalking into position to do the same to him. There was nowhere to run, even if he could have run, which was hardly his strong suit.

"Deena?" he called in a tremulous voice.

"Yeah," she answered. "We in deep shit now, baby."

164 EAST 64ST STREET

HE WAS DOODLING with some field incantations that were proving especially thorny when he noticed a blob of light dancing in mid-air a little to the right of the dinette table. He recognized it for what it was, and answered the ''Are you receiving visitors?'' query by tracing a simple pattern with his finger.

The blob of light wafted closer, drifting over the carpet. It stopped and grew brighter, suddenly unfolding and spreading out to take the shape of a human figure, that of a beautiful woman.

''Hi, Ferne.''

''Incarnadine.'' His sister's greeting came with a cheery smile.

He sat back and took her in. She was as pretty as ever, dark of eye and delicate of face, her hair a dark waterfall spilling to her shoulders. She wore a crimson velvet gown, ornamented in gold filigree. The garment left her shoulders bare. Her skin was very white, very pure, totally unblemished. There were wild highlights in her eyes, and over them an ironic, skeptical downturn to her brow.

''Where are you?'' he asked.

''The castle. Deems told me where you are, and I can scarcely believe it.''

''It's about time somebody did something about re-establishing the gateway to Earth.''

"Yes, it was long overdue," she said.

"I haven't done it yet, though."

"No?" One dark eyebrow rose. "But you're close?"

"Another few days. The problems have been tricky, but I think I have most of them solved."

"Good. Then we'll be seeing you soon."

"I hope. You said Deems told you. Were you in Albion?"

"Yes, I just happened to drop into my estate there. I'm having the house remodeled, and I had to consult with the master carpenter."

"Odd. Deems appeared to be unaware of your having any permanent residence in Albion."

"Is he? He should be aware. I've never made any secret of it. But, then, I rarely tell Deems my business. May I sit down?"

"I'm terribly sorry. I'd offer you a chair—" He smiled. "—But of course, you're not really here."

"Don't trouble yourself." She reached out and made as if to grasp something, pulling it near. She lowered herself to a sitting position. What she sat on was completely invisible. She arranged the folds of her gown and leaned back. "There. Now we can have a nice chat. As I was saying, my estate isn't exactly in Deems' kingdom, it's in the Protectorate of Westphalen—next door. These days it's only nominally a protectorate, and Deems has little power there, aside from receiving an annual tribute. I've had the place for years, and I don't visit as often as I'd like."

"How did Deems find you?"

She shrugged. "I don't know. I got a message from him by special courier this morning. The note said you had requested that I call you immediately on the Universal Projector. It sounded important, so I threw a few things in a bag and got to the portal as fast as I could. And here I am, back at the castle and on the line to you, just as you requested. What's all the fuss?"

"I'm afraid Deems made it sound more urgent than it really was. I merely wanted to talk with you, Ferne."

"Well, I'm delighted, of course, and it's been much too long since we last had a nice, cozy chat. . . ." She batted her long eyelashes at him. "But there must be a little more to it than that."

"A bit more, I have to admit. Before I get to it, do you mind if I slide a chair under your image? I find it strangely unsettling to have unsupported bodies levitating about."

"Feel free."

He got up and fetched a dinette chair, positioning it so that it looked convincing in the part. "That's a little better," he said, resuming his seat. "Now, what I wanted to ask you is this. Somebody's been fooling around at the castle. Is it you?"

Her face remained expressionless for a moment. Then she threw back her head and laughed. "Oh, Inky, the word 'blunt' was invented for you. That's always been your favorite tactic, hasn't it? You always lay your cards right on the table. No bluffing, no subtlety, nothing."

"Yes, at first. When the tactic fails, as it usually does, then I get sneaky."

"Yes, I've noticed over the years that this is your usual opening gambit. But why, if it usually avails you nothing?"

"I didn't say it availed me nothing. I can get a lot out of reactions. I like to read them, weigh them. The emotional overtones to any reaction, however insincere or pretended, are always very interesting. And very informative."

"Really? Fascinating. And *my* reaction—just now?"

"Oh, very interesting indeed."

She smiled. "And informative, I hope."

"That laugh spoke volumes."

The smile faded. She seemed concerned. "And what did it tell you?"

He crossed his legs, chuckling.

She frowned. "I think you're making it all up." She studied his face. "Yes, you're bluffing. Making me think you have one up on me already, and we haven't even really begun to bargain."

"Bargain? Are we at odds, in some way?"

She lifted her delicate shoulders. "Haven't we always been?"

He considered it, nodding. "Well, yes, it does seem to me that we've butted heads one or two times over the years. Just why, I can't imagine, because I've never had anything but the fondest regards for you, dear sister."

"And I for you, dear brother." Her expression hardened. "Now let's cut the crap and get down to business."

He laughed. "I really didn't know we had any business." He laughed again. "I suppose I can totally discount the first two minutes of this conversation. All that stuff about getting a message, coming to the castle. What exactly have you been up to, Ferne?"

She sat up and looked straight at him. "Never mind that. Listen to me. Your castle has been invaded. Successfully, I might add.

What remains of your Guardsmen are prisoners or deserters. Most of them are of the latter category, having fled through sundry aspects.''

"As per their standing orders in case of a successful incursion into the castle," he said calmly.

"Of course. Very wise, actually, as they had no chance."

"Who are the invaders?"

"They originate from an aspect that Dad sealed off long ago, on a hunch that the inhabitants might be potential troublemakers. He was right."

"Well, now," he said, scratching his chin. "That could be any one of about a hundred aspects that Dad had doubts about."

"Does it really matter which one? They are a race of bipeds, very warlike, very aggrandizing. Overwhelmingly so. They discovered the gateway quite readily, and instantly realized the unparalleled strategic value of the castle."

He nodded. "Gateway to thousands of worlds ripe for conquest."

"Yes. And they have technology, good technology. And a little magic, too; more, since they've been in the castle. So no worlds are safe from them."

"They sound like a real going concern." He shifted in his seat and recrossed his legs. "Looks like you're putting your cards on the table, for once. I thought we'd be here for hours, playing cat and mouse."

"It would have been fun, but . . ." She gave him a sulky look. "Damn it, Inky, you have a way of putting me off my stride. That 'reading reactions' business was just a ploy to get me to think that you have something on me, when, in fact, the situation is entirely the reverse."

"You have something on me?"

"You're locked out, dear brother. On the outside looking in. You're in New York, and you'll never be able to summon the gateway to the castle, let alone stabilize it in a New York apartment. I have established the gateway. Elsewhere."

"So, you *have* been fooling about here. With Trent?"

She chuckled gloatingly. "I knew you'd fall for that. You detected meddling and instantly suspected Trent, so you hied yourself to Earth to check him out. And he was as oily and as sneaky as always, and looking worried about your showing up there after all these years, nosing about. So you thought, 'Trent is up to something.' And he may very well be, if I know Trent. But it doesn't have anything to do with what I'm doing.''

"Brilliant so far, sis. By the way, did I tell you that you're absolutely stunning in that dress?''

"Thank you.'' She reddened slightly. "Damn you! You always know exactly what to say to bring me up short. That's why I'm not inclined to toy with you, Inky. You are much too dangerous for that, and I'm not ashamed to admit it.''

"I see.'' He looked down, tapping one shoe against the other. "So, you've taken over Castle Perilous.''

"Oh, not yet. We're only in the first stage of things.''

"You're not in cahoots with these invaders?''

She wrinkled her nose in disgust. "They're perfectly dreadful beasts, and I wouldn't think of having anything personally to do with them.''

"So you just busted the containing spell and let them spill out into the castle? Unwise, Ferne honey. Unwise.''

"On the contrary, they've been very useful. They are a bargaining chip.''

"Indeed? Tell me this. Just where are you in the castle, if the castle has been invaded?''

"Well, you don't think I wouldn't take precautions, do you? We've sealed off the old family residence. We're quite safe here, for the moment.''

"I see. So the Albion aspect is protected.''

"Naturally. And the Earth aspect is here, too, stabilized nicely. And the door is locked, Inky. Only I have the key.''

"What did you mean by calling the invaders a bargaining chip? What are you bargaining for?''

"For a share of control of the castle. And its power.''

"Of course. And you want to bargain with me.''

"Who else, my liege lord?''

"Why do I figure in at all?'' he asked. "According to you, I'm locked out.''

"We need you.''

"Who is 'we'?''

"Deems and I,'' Ferne said.

He looked off, nodding, understanding. "I see. Old Deems is finally having second thoughts about abdicating in favor of me. Why, I wonder?''

She laughed mirthlessly. "He doesn't want the throne. Through his profligacy and general ineptitude, he's screwed up things in Albion to the point where he finally had to ask me for help. Magical help. The kingdom's in a mess. Fiscally speaking, he's just about at the end of his rope."

Incarnadine folded his arms and nodded. "So, he wasn't kidding."

"Deems has trouble lying. There's no guile in the man at all. And not a great deal of brains. Imagine him trying to pretend that he didn't know how to reach me. Dead giveaway."

"You're right. I knew immediately that you and he were up to something. But by then it was too late. I was here, and, as you put it, on the outside looking in."

"You couldn't have timed things any better. I had no idea when the creatures would make their move to take over Perilous, but I had hoped you would follow the Trent lead and go to New York before the attack. And you went, beating them by about two days. It was a little close, but it worked out. Had you been present during the invasion, I don't think it would have made much difference. But your not being there was good insurance."

Incarnadine got up and went to the dry bar. He poured himself two fingers of whiskey, then tore the cap off a small bottle of club soda and mixed it in. "I'd offer you a drink, but . . ."

"I'm having one served to me here," she said, holding an invisible glass. The faint suggestion of a long-stemmed wineglass—a milky, wavering outline—took form in her hand as she brought it to her lips.

"I've often wondered," he said, "why the spell that projects the image won't project any other material thing but the subject's clothes. Why just clothes?"

"Dad's sense of propriety, I guess. How would it look, me sitting here in front of my brother naked?"

"Well, it wouldn't look all that bad," he said. "All in the family, you know."

"Inky, I'm surprised," she said coyly. "I never knew you harbored incestuous thoughts."

He feigned shock. "Hold your scandalous tongue, woman! That would be unspeakable. Not to say bad form. No, dear, chaste sister, I simply have always thought that you were a knockout. Purely a matter of aesthetics." He took a drink and walked back to the chair and sat down.

She shook her head. "You're just sandbagging me again. Forget it, Inky. It won't work."

"Ferne, your biggest fault is that you can't take a compliment."

"That may be. I'm much too suspicious to accept them at face value."

"Pity," he said. "But back to business. You say you need me. For what?"

"We need your Guardsmen to take back the castle. Deems' forces aren't adequate. Only you know where your boys are hiding. With them and Deems' army combined—and with a little help from the Recondite Arts—we'll be able to stuff the disgusting little devils back into their hole."

"You hope!"

Ferne shrugged. "I don't see why it can't be done. The invaders are troublesomely adept at fighting, true, but they're certainly not invincible. See here. You thwarted Prince Vorn and destroyed the combined military might of the Hunran Empire and its allies. Surely you and Deems can turn back an army that has but one access way into the castle! Close off the portal, and reinforcements and supplies are denied them! Then it becomes merely a question of mopping up."

He rolled his eyes. "Thank you, Karl von Clausewitz!"

"Oh, really, Inky, you're always carping over details. You'll think of something, I'm sure."

He took a good stiff drink. "Okay, say Deems and I beat back this horde of—what the hell do they look like, anyway? Want to give me a hint?"

"Disgusting, squat blue creatures with nasty teeth and big, flat webbed feet." She turned up her nose as she brought the ghost wineglass to her lips. "Horrible things, really."

Frowning, he massaged his forehead. "Gods. That rings a bell somewhere."

"Again, what does it matter? Their magic is primitive, and their technology won't work in the castle—"

"But they will undoubtedly establish bases through some of the portals. Once they fan out, they'll be unbeatable. Like termites in an old barn. Ferne, you don't know what you've done."

"I don't believe you."

"Of course you don't. Anyway, as I was saying, let's assume Deems and I do prevail and win back the castle. What's to prevent me from kicking Deems and his rabble out, and you along with them?''

"I'll simply 'bust' another containment spell and let more termites into the barn.''

"Not if I see that you never set foot in Perilous again.''

She smiled serenely. "You can't keep me out, Inky.''

He sat back and emitted a grudging snort. "You're probably right.'' He drained his glass and set it aside. "So—after this great victory, you, Deems, and I will make a cozy triumvirate. Eh?''

"I think it sounds very friendly. Various contingents of Deems' forces will stay on to complement select units of your Guardsmen. The two forces will share duties equally.''

Incarnadine rose and approached the figure of his sister.

"No, Ferne. It won't work. No deal.''

"Think again, Inky. You can't get back. You can't summon the gateway now. The end on your side is nailed down in a remote spot. Even if it weren't, I very much doubt you could re-establish the portal. You said you had run into some difficulties.''

"I admit it," he said. "It's a tough problem. I've been studying as much high-energy physics as magic.''

"Exactly. It was only after years of study that I finally found a solution.''

"You've been spending quite a good deal of time here, haven't you?''

"Oh, yes. Once I found I could summon the gateway from this side, I began dividing my time between there and Albion. I prefer the latter, by the way, but Earth is a dandy place to build up your magical muscles. Earth magic is the most powerful of all, precisely because it's the most difficult to work with, and to master.''

"You can say that again. Still, it's no deal, sis. The only thing that doesn't make sense was that attempt on my life.''

She fixed him in a questioning stare. "I can't imagine what you're talking about.''

"Really? Well, somebody tried to take me out. I'll admit, you make a dubious suspect. From what you say, you'd stand to lose by my death—at least for now. Once the castle's back in our hands, it'll be another matter. Then I'll simply be a liability.''

"I repeat, I don't know what you're talking about. You have a limited amount of time, my brother. You said it yourself—once the invaders establish a beachhead, they'll be hard to dislodge. Perilous will be a lost cause.''

"And it will be on your head."

She shrugged. "The decision is yours. Share Perilous, and it will stand. Insist on being stubborn, and the Haplodites will have to find a new home."

He shook his head sadly. "Sister, I'm disappointed in you. I never thought you would stoop so low."

"Oh, stuff it. Look, Inky. Just say the word and I'll let you through, and we can get on with business."

"What does Deems get out of this?"

"Gold for his royal treasury. What else?"

"Oh, no," he groaned. "Ferne, I'm surprised at you. You know very well that Albion is the wrong kind of universe for alchemical changes. The stuff you'll whip up for him will turn phony in a matter of months."

"Who will care but Deems' creditors? And who will believe them?"

"Ferne, you shouldn't go around screwing up the economy of a world like that! You're talking about a lot of gold, aren't you? If I know Deems, you are."

She waved the matter aside. "It is of no moment whatsoever."

He sighed and sat down. "No deal, Ferne."

Her eyes flashed. "Then you'll rot there, little brother!"

He flipped a palm over. "New York is not exactly Siberia."

"Have fun, Inky. Take in a Broadway show or two. There are still some fine restaurants in New York. You might try Windows on the Park. It's at the top of the Gulf & Western building. The food is good and the view is breathtaking."

"I'll be sure to check it out."

"You'll be sorry, Incarnadine. I'll give you twenty-four hours to deal. After that, Perilous is a lost cause."

"I think I know what you're up to, Ferne."

"You couldn't possibly," she said. "Good-bye, Inky."

"Good-bye, Ferne."

Her figure collapsed to a ball of light, then was gone. The useless chair stood in the middle of the floor, as empty now of form as content.

He sat for a long while, silently contemplating areas of the walls and ceiling.

Keep—Near the South Tower

"THIS LOOKS PROMISING," Gene said as he peered across the threshold of an attractive aspect. There was sunshine out there, and green grass, some trees, and a small pond. It looked like the grazing meadow of a small farm, *sans* cattle. He sniffed the air and could have sworn he smelled fresh-cut hay. But there were no buildings visible, and something told him this was not an inhabited aspect.

"Trouble is," he added, "it'll look just as inviting to the Bluefaces."

Linda said, "Maybe we'll be safe if we get far enough away from the portal."

"But we don't want to get too far away from the castle. We might not be able to make it back."

"True. But we haven't found a better aspect so far. Aren't those apple trees over there?"

"Maybe," Gene said. "Looks like the wrong season for apples, though. I vote no. Anyone disagree?"

No one did. Gene and Linda walked away from the portal, Snowclaw and Sheila following.

"At least we haven't seen Bluefaces for a good while," Sheila commented.

"Damn, I wish I knew what I was looking for," Gene said, preoccupied with his thoughts.

"What would you be looking for," Linda asked, "if you knew what you were looking for?"

"An aspect that could turn up some kind of fancy, high-tech weapon that would be effective against the Bluefaces."

"The way I understand it," Sheila said, "technology doesn't work in the castle."

"Depends on what you mean by technology," Gene said. "I've heard tell of aspects where it's pretty hard to tell magic from technology. Maybe something from one of those worlds would do the trick."

"Everybody keeps saying that there are some pretty weird aspects," Linda said. "Maybe we'll get lucky."

"Fat chance," Gene said glumly. "I think we're sunk. We've lost the castle."

"It wasn't ours to begin with," Linda said.

"No, but it was the only home we had."

Sheila said, "My usual luck. I just start getting used to the place, and we get chased out. Thing is, I can't decide whether it's any great loss."

"The castle's a mixed blessing, Sheila," Gene said. "But it's given me one thing I lacked back in the real world. Adventure. Real, heart-pounding, thrill-a-minute, no-holds-barred adventure. They don't make that in the mundane world. They just make boredom, periodically relieved by stark terror."

Another aperture appeared suddenly in the wall ahead, this one revealing a scene of dense jungle. Gene halted in his tracks and put out an arm to hold his companions back.

"Wait a minute. This looks like trouble."

They stood and watched. Birdcalls echoed in the treetops, the undergrowth rustled here and fidgeted there, and tropical sun streamed green and gold through the high jungle canopy. But not much else happened.

"What were you saying about heart-pounding adventure?" Linda asked.

"Yeah . . . well." Gene pushed his broadsword back into its scabbard. "We're really getting the proverbial horns of the dilemma right in the butt. If we hide out in one of these wild aspects, we'll be safe from the Bluefaces, all right. But you can bet the damn thing'll close up and leave us stranded."

"Great choice," Linda said. "Die in some weird place, or stay here and get taken prisoner." She gave a tiny shudder. "If they take prisoners. I wonder if they think humans are good to eat."

Snowclaw said, "I've often wondered myself."

The great white beast's hairless companions regarded him gravely.

Abstractedly Snowclaw stroked the blade of the huge longsword that Linda had conjured for him. Then he flashed his teeth, chuckling impishly. "Just kidding, friends."

"Maybe we'll just have to take the chance and hole up in one of these," Sheila said, pointing toward the jungle.

"It's a thought," Gene said. "But not this one. We need one with some signs of civilization."

"That, I think, is going to be hard," Linda said. "Did you ever notice that most aspects are either uninhabited, deserted, or, if they do have civilization, it's primitive?"

Gene thought about it. "Yeah, now that you mention it. I've seen some strange things, briefly glimpsed through aspects here and there. But for the most part, you're right. If the aspect is easily accessible, there's usually nothing there except picture-postcard stuff. Pretty, but of no use. There must be a reason for it."

"Just think if the portal to Earth were, say, in the middle of New York City."

"Right, this castle would be co-op apartments by now. Maybe that's the reason that portals to worlds with advanced civilizations are so rare. Maybe the castle was designed that way in order to protect it from invasion from within, so to speak."

"Makes sense," Linda said.

"Come on, let's get going."

They moved away from the jungle aspect. Farther down the corridor they passed two large empty halls, one at either hand.

Gene thought awhile, then said, "Yeah, it makes sense. But what happened with the Bluefaces? Did the castle's defenses—whatever they are—break down? Or does this kind of thing happen periodically?"

"If this place is as old as they say it is," Linda said, "it would have been invaded long ago."

Gene shrugged. "Maybe it was. Maybe Lord Incarnadine is an invader himself."

"Haven't you ever talked to any of the servants? They all say—"

"Yeah, I know. They all say Incarnadine's been lord of Perilous for hundreds of years. And before that his dad was lord for a thousand years. I know—I'm just throwing hypotheses against the wall and seeing if any of 'em leave a stain.'' He ruminated for a few more paces. ''Thing is, I *have* seen cities and high-tech-looking stuff through a few of the floating aspects, most of which look mighty hard to cross.'' He shook his head slowly. ''I can't figure it out.''

''Halt!''

They had just begun to cross through an intersecting tunnel. Swords already drawn, four Bluefaces were double-timing down the left branch, breaking into a charge when Gene and his companions came into view.

''Run!'' Gene yelled, turning Sheila around and shoving her back down the corridor. Linda and Snowclaw needed no prompting. They ran, passing the two empty halls and the jungle aspect, but before they reached the crossing passageway ahead, three more Bluefaces turned the corner, snarling and waving swords.

Linda skidded to a stop. She had less than five seconds to arrive at a magical solution to the problem. She fought an urge to panic and closed her eyes, hoping the decision she made would be the right one.

Snowclaw turned to fight the first group of Bluefaces and Gene raced to meet the threesome. Snowy's first victory was swift. His left hand struck like the head of a snake, tearing out the throat of the leader. He neatly sidestepped the falling body to bring his longsword to bear on the second creature.

Sheila backed against the wall and squatted, hands covering her head, mind gone numb with fear. Peeking between fingers, she saw Gene clash swords with two Bluefaces as a third maneuvered for position in the narrow hallway. Gene held his own for a spell, but three-on-one proved too much even for Gene's expert swordcraft. He backstepped, fending off all three now, parrying and riposting, his blade a silver blur. Snowy was similarly boxed in, his three opponents giving him a hard time.

Then something strange happened. Sheila blinked her eyes and looked again. Either she was seeing triple, or there were three Genes. And Snowclaw seemed to have suddenly acquired two comrades-in-arms who looked exactly like him.

With a helpless groan, Sheila covered her eyes again as the *whang* and *clank* of swordplay filled the corridor. When she looked again, the situation was even more confused. Now there were more Bluefaces, and still more duplicates of Gene and Snowclaw.

"A duel between us, sorceress!" one Blueface called out. He was standing back from the melee, and appeared to be speaking to Linda, who stood calmly in the middle of things.

"You got it, Blueface!" Linda answered. She stuck her tongue out.

From that point on, things got very bizarre indeed. The number of combatants seemed to increase every few seconds. In a short time the passageway became the scene of an armed engagement of major proportions, spilling over into the great rooms on either side. New sorts of combatants appeared: knights in armor, Roman legionnaires, and Greek hoplites crossed swords with an outrageous assortment of monsters. Tentacles snaked, talons raked, and claws tore, all to the tune of singing steel. The noise was deafening. Sheila dove to the floor and flattened herself against the wall. When someone or something stepped on her ankle, she gave a yelp and crawled off.

Someone grabbed her arm and yanked her halfway up. It was Gene.

"Get to the aspect and jump through!" he yelled. "And keep down!" He let her go.

Sheila crawled, keeping her head down but watching out for stamping feet and other, stranger extremities. She was kicked once in the leg, then took the heel of a boot in her ribs. She doubled up with pain; and then got her foot mashed. Whimpering, she rose to a crouch and hobbled away. She stumbled, fell, and got up again.

Someone seized her wrist and spun her around. It was a Blueface, sword raised and ready to strike. Sheila stood transfixed, hypnotized by the gleaming blade above her. She had never really considered what it would be like to be struck by a sword. The blade was huge and looked wickedly sharp, sharper than the Japanese knife in those ubiquitous TV commercials where the guy cuts a beer can open and then dices an avocado. She was now up against the awful prospect, the impending reality, of having that blade slice through her flesh. The amazing thing was that she couldn't scream. She simply stood there in this frozen instant, acutely conscious of her fate, almost dispassionately wondering if there would be much pain.

She never got the opportunity to find out. Another blade flashed round from behind and took the creature's head clean off, leaving its neck a pulsing fountain of purple blood. Almost in slow motion, the body dropped at her feet. Snowclaw—which one?—grabbed her arm and shoved her in the direction of the portal.

"Move, Sheila!"

She ran, but more fighting blocked her way. She cut to the right, sidestepped left, then stooped and ducked between the legs of a strange giant creature covered in yellow feathers. The incongruous thought of *Sesame Street's* Big Bird came to her, unbidden, as she caught sight of an opening and sprinted for the portal.

She tripped over something and fell. A man in tunic and crested bronze helmet helped her to her feet, then saluted with his sword, turned, and rejoined the fighting. Sheila looked down at the body she had tripped over.

It was Gene, and he was dead, his skull split open and a huge gash in his neck. Sheila screamed and kept screaming.

Someone took her arm and shook her violently.

It was Gene. "Let's go!"

Dumbfounded, she swung her gaze back and forth between Gene's twin bodies, living and dead.

"Forget it!" he said. "Come on!"

As she was being dragged down the corridor, she couldn't take her eyes off Gene's paradoxical dead body. But she soon lost sight of it as the battle closed in around her. The next few seconds were lost to complete disorientation. Then there was light and a sudden wave of heat—it was like running out of an air-conditioned building on a blistering-hot day. The castle was gone and she was outside, in the middle of a humid and fragrant rain forest. The portal was an upright rectangle, like an odd movie screen, standing in the undergrowth, and through it she could see inside the castle. The fighting raged on.

"Run! Hide!"

Gene was shaking her, yelling into her ear.

"Get lost! Run!"

She was about to ask about Linda when she was rendered speechless by the sight of Gene's form suddenly growing blurred and indistinct. Then he disappeared altogether, and she was left standing alone. Astonished, she whirled around, again and again, her bewildered eyes searching frantically for any sight of him.

But he was gone. He had simply vanished.

He reappeared just as quickly. He and Linda came through the gateway at a run.

But before Sheila could register shock, they disappeared as inexplicably as the first Gene had done.

They were followed by Snowclaw, who also vanished without fanfare and without a trace. Two more of Snowclaw's doppelgangers repeated the trick, each blinking out of existence shortly after crossing the threshold.

Then another Gene-and-Linda set came through. This one did not disappear.

"Here she is!" Gene yelled as he ran by. "Let's go, Sheila!"

He grabbed Sheila's arm and dragged her along. Sheila tripped, staggered, then found her footing. Gene let go of her arm and she ran after them.

Eventually they pulled ahead and she lost them in the sea of vegetation. She dashed on through the thick undergrowth, leafy tentacles grabbing at her feet, overhanging vines whipping at her face and snagging her clothing. She stopped and looked wildly about. Someone grabbed her sleeve and yanked her down.

It was Gene, crouched with Linda behind some bushes.

"Shhh!"

Sheila peered back at the portal. As she watched, several Bluefaces crossed over and promptly dematerialized. Then Snowclaw came running through. Apparently he was the genuine article. He stayed hugely real.

Gene jumped up and waved at him, whistling.

Snowclaw caught sight of Gene and started forward. A Blueface came charging out of the portal, saw Snowclaw, and jumped him from behind. Snowclaw rolled to the ground to avoid a wicked slash, and in so doing, shot out a foot to trip the creature up. The Blueface went down. There was a brief scuffle on the ground, then both creatures sprang to their feet, swords flashing in the tropical sunlight.

By the time Gene got there to help, the Blueface lay on the ground, wanting the top half of its skull. Gene led Snowy back to the hiding spot.

The foursome watched the portal for five full minutes. No one else came out. All was quiet.

"Maybe that last one was the only survivor," Gene said. "The only real one, that is." He found a tree trunk and leaned against it. "How are you guys?"

Linda said, "I wasn't in much danger. That Blueface was a

strong magician, though. If we hadn't ducked out, I don't know."
She shook her head ruefully.

"Sheila?"

Horror-struck, she was staring at Gene. "Gene, I . . . I *saw*
you. You were—"

"Yeah, I know. It was pretty interesting."

Sheila's mouth hung open. She worked her jaws, trying to form
words in reply.

Gene shrugged. "Well, philosophically speaking—"

Sheila burst into tears, and presently she found that Gene was
holding her. She hugged him, pressing her face against the braided
leather of his breastplate.

"It's okay, it's okay," Gene was saying, but she knew that
nothing would ever be the same again.

"Oh, no!"

Blinking back tears, Sheila looked at Linda.

Linda's face was ashen. "The portal's gone," she said.

EAST 64TH AND LEXINGTON

TRENT'S MERCEDES SWOOPED to the curb and halted beneath a sign that read NO STOPPING ANYTIME. Trent got out and opened the trunk. Incarnadine threw his luggage in; then they both got in the car.

It was about three-thirty on a Friday afternoon, and traffic was already congealing into a hopeless clot. Trent drove south on Lexington to 58th Street and turned west.

"Think we can get through the Lincoln Tunnel in under an hour?" Incarnadine asked.

"Sure, no problem," Trent answered with the casual self-confidence that only a New Yorker can muster in the face of impending gridlock.

"I'd be willing to bet we never make it to the tunnel. This town was always bad, traffic-wise, but the situation seems to have reached absurd proportions."

"Come now, you're exaggerating."

Incarnadine laughed. "You really have become a native."

Trent shrugged. "Maybe." He dodged and weaved expertly through the taxi-thick rush, applying the car's horn in liberal doses. "Tell me again why I should help you."

Incarnadine sighed and leaned back in the leather seat. "I don't think I want to go through it again. If you can't marshal enough reasons on your own, your heart's probably not in it. If that's the case, let me off here, and we'll say no more about it.''

"Hold your horses, I'm not backing out. I just want to hear again why I should take your side against Ferne. And Deems, though I don't hold a brief for him.''

"I'm not asking you to take my side. I'm enlisting your aid in a campaign to save Perilous from the irresponsible machinations of our crazy sister. She's really gone off the deep end this time, Trent.''

"You say she has something else in mind besides sharing power with you and Deems?''

"She wants to be nothing less than mistress of Perilous. She's wanted it for years, and has stated so to me on a number of occasions. Always with a laugh, mind you, and a pretty smile, as if she didn't mean it.''

"Always. That's our Ferne. But who am I to thwart her ambitions? Look, Inky. I've lived in this culture long enough to have been influenced by certain so-called progressive ideas. In our world, as in this one, women traditionally get the short end of the stick when it comes to things like royal succession. She's older than you, but you are a male, and she was passed over. You inherited the Seat Perilous, the crown, and the castle. She's pissed about that, as rightly she should be.''

"In the moral universe you're delineating, our sister Dorcas, as oldest sibling, should have taken the throne upon Dad's death.''

"Dorcas is traditional-minded as hell, and you know it. She'd be on your side, for Christ's sake. Let's forget hypotheticals. It's Ferne who thinks she has a civil rights case.''

"Ferne may have a case, but the way she's going about redressing her grievance is guaranteed to put more than Castle Perilous in jeopardy.''

"Not if you gave in a little and let her share power.''

"Can't be done, Trent. I mean, we're not talking about political power in the traditional sense here, are we?''

"Well, not exactly," Trent said. "As far as Perilous' local situation is concerned, the Pale is a wasteland, and has been for centuries. Is there anyone at all living out there on the plains these days?''

"There are about two hundred tenant farmers and their families left, scraping by as always. They won't live in the castle for religious reasons.''

"Only two hundred? Gods! Then the Pale is virtually deserted outside the castle. No, we're not speaking of governing a few hundred square *zeln* of marginal farmland. It's a matter of controlling whole worlds—at least potentially."

"Trent, you know Perilous can't control worlds. Not very well, at any rate. For instance, take this one. Could we rule Earth from Perilous?"

"Maybe not a complex, heavily populated world where magic is problematical. But other, simpler aspects where the ground rules are a trifle more liberal? Yes indeedy. We could run worlds like those."

"Why? To what purpose?"

Trent swerved to avoid a cab that had cut in front to pick up a fare. He chuckled. "Why? Something to do. Something different. A new kick. A little excitement to leaven the boredom that's inevitable in the lives of long-lived sorts such as we."

"You might take up batiking. Or beer can collecting. How about aerobics? Maybe holistic medicine?"

"Okay, okay. I was simply trying to see it from Ferne's point of view."

"I think I know what her point of view is," Incarnadine said. "She's nuts. Gone round the bend. Crackers."

"What makes you think that?"

"I'm pretty sure she intends to make a deal with the Hosts of Hell."

Trent honked angrily at a brave pedestrian, a man in a trench coat and wool cap, who had stepped out in front of the car. The man jumped back to the curb in the nick of time as Trent roared by. Incarnadine heard shouted obscenities dwindling in the car's wake.

"How do you know?" Trent said.

"I don't, for sure," Incarnadine answered, "but I'm fairly sure she tried to have me killed, and that means she's not dealing squarely with Deems. I don't think Deems would go along with assassinating me."

"Unless he is as desperate as Ferne said he was."

"Possibly. But I don't think Ferne wants to share power with anyone, let alone Deems, let alone me. She needs allies to take and hold the castle, and I think she thinks that only supernatural allies will do. She's probably right. Alone, she'd have to face her subjects, to say nothing of the Guard. And there's always the Guests as a wild card. And all of them are magicians, to varying degrees. That's what makes Perilous a fun place and makes plotters toss and turn all night. I do myself, sometimes.''

"This all sounds complicated," Trent said uneasily. "Why is she stringing Deems along? Why does she need him?''

"If she had simply summoned the Hosts of Hell to take over the castle, Deems would have thrown in with me to fight them off. So would Dorcas, and, I think, even you.''

Trent seemed to be grinning in spite of himself. "But I was stranded here, remember? Still am, as a matter of fact.''

"Bullshit, Trent. I never believed it for one minute.''

Trent laughed. "Okay, I never was good at keeping secrets.''

"You shouldn't have shown off at dinner, when you let me see how you do your aging act. Obviously you've learned to adapt to this universe. How long did it take you to learn how to summon the gateway?''

"Oh, about five years, as I said. But once I could do it, I had no interest in going back to Perilous, or in living in any other universe but this one. I simply had settled down here and wasn't about to move. I have friends here, you know. I've put down roots.''

Incarnadine nodded, looking out the window. Traffic thickened up even more as they reached the West Side.

"I still don't quite understand it," Trent said. "Okay, she wouldn't have won any popularity contests by teaming up with a bunch of demons. But can any of us prevail against the Hosts of Hell, singly or combined?''

"I don't know. The Hosts of Hell are a troublesome bunch.''

"That's putting it mildly. If Dad feared anything at all, it was those guys. He warned us about them more than once.''

"Dad knew their power. It's not for nothing that the strongest containment spell in the castle is the one blocking their aspect.'' Incarnadine rubbed his dark beard. He was glad not to have to go about in makeup all the time. Only his C. Wainwright Smithton persona required his looking elderly. "As I said, I don't know exactly what Ferne's up to. But I'm sure I'll find out sooner or later. As I take my dying breath, maybe.'' He opened his coat and loosened the collar of his shirt. "Tell me this. Why *are* you helping me? Or are you?''

Trent took a long breath. "I guess it's occurred to you that I could be behind all this.''

"Yes, it has. Forget it. That's a possibility I'll have to live with. I'm betting you aren't. Granted that you're not conspiring with

Ferne or running her, why help me find the portal and get back to Perilous?"

"Because I don't want Perilous taken over by militaristic blue monsters," Trent said, "let alone demonic entities from some fever-dream universe who would rule Creation if they could get their claws on it."

"Makes sense. Another question. How sure are you about Ferne's having an estate in western Pennsylvania?"

"I thought you'd found out. You were the one who asked me about it."

"It was just a wild hunch. We've been getting a lot of Guests from that area lately."

"Well, it was a pretty good hunch. I've known about it for some time."

"How did you find out?"

"About ten years ago I woke up in the middle of the night with the strongest feeling that someone was doing major magic in this universe. I didn't have the vaguest notion of how to locate the source, so I worked on that problem awhile. Eventually I came up with a direction-finding technique, and the next time I got that same feeling, I went out in the car and got a triangulation fix on it. Over the years, I've managed to get a wider baseline and pinpointed it pretty accurately."

"What's the name of the town it's near, again?"

"Ligonier, Pennsylvania."

"That's where the portal ought to be nailed down."

"You would think. But the booby traps and fortifications around it are going to be a living nightmare."

Incarnadine nodded, smiling thinly. "Let's deal with the horrors as they come. First we have to survive the Lincoln Tunnel and the New Jersey Turnpike."

They ate at a Burger King on the Pennsylvania Turnpike near Reading. It was about eight o'clock, and the night was cold and dark.

"What's with the gadget?" Trent asked as he munched his Whopper.

"Checking some parameters," Incarnadine said as he tapped with one finger on the keys of a pocket computer. "Stresses, field strengths, other variables. I can't keep track of them by feel here."

"That's the first thing you've got to learn. You can't use

technology as a crutch here. Otherwise your magic becomes a sort of pseudoscience.''

Incarnadine smiled ruefully. "I know what you mean. But getting an intuitive grip on things is going to take a little more time. For me, at least.''

"Don't worry, you'll get it eventually.''

"I hope I get it before I get it, if you take my meaning.''

"You haven't touched your french fries.''

"I can't get used to this kind of food. Ring Lardner once told me that American culture could only get more bland and homogenized as time went on, and he was right.''

"I like American food,'' Trent said. "It's fast, nice and greasy, and appeals to the kid in us all.''

"Nothing wrong with hamburgers and fried potatoes. It's just that—uh, never mind. Can we go?''

"Of course.''

They walked out into the brisk winter night. The parking lot was well lighted near the restaurant, but Trent had parked on the dim outskirts under a burnt-out light.

"Ring Lardner?'' Trent said. "You were always one to hobnob with the literati.''

"Forever courting the Muse's favored. I liked the old Algonquin Round Table crowd, back in the twenties and thirties. Those were the days.''

"Who was that writer woman you had a fling with back then?''

"Dorothy Parker? Very briefly. She was fun, but she had a melancholy streak in her. You know, she once said to me—''

A windshield shattered in front of them, its sound almost masking the dull thud of a silenced gunshot that came from behind. Incarnadine dove over a hood, slid off the fender, hit concrete, and rolled to a crouch. He listened, seeing nothing. He heard running footsteps recede. Then a car door slammed, and tires squealed. He peeked over the front end of an Audi and saw a dark nondescript sedan peeling out of the lot. It screeched onto the turnpike re-entry ramp and sped away.

Trent came over, holding a compact submachine gun. He handed it to Incarnadine.

"You keep this. They could be laying for us down the road.''

Incarnadine examined the weapon, then clicked on the safety and folded up the wire stock. "I guess this puts you in the clear.''

"Maybe. I could have had one of my guys stage it.''

"Possible, but unlikely."

"You're right." Trent yawned. "Let's go. We have a five-hour drive ahead of us."

"You look tired. Want me to drive?"

"When was the last time you drove an automobile?"

"1958, I think," Incarnadine said. "Why?"

"I have a pretty good autopilot spell. We can both nap. We're going to need some sleep before we tackle Ferne's place."

"Do you trust the spell?"

"It drives better than I do," Trent said. "Besides, I belong to the Triple-A. They'll tow the wreckage away, no charge."

"In that case, start with the hocus-pocus, O great Trentino."

ELSEWHERE

DEENA STROKED THE shaggy mane of the animal she called Buster.
The hair was thick, soft, and smooth. Buster looked at her with
huge golden cat-eyes and communicated warm feelings of friendli-
ness, bordering on affection. Certain filaments of the strange and
complex organ which blossomed antlerlike from Buster's head
appeared to undulate slightly. The organ, a light pink in color,
looked somewhat like a stand of coral, with fine, featherlike hair
covering some of the thinner tendrils.

"Yeah, I like you, too, Buster," Deena said. "I started to like
you when I found out you wasn't gonna eat me."

Barnaby lay in the grass with his head resting on the tawny flank
of the one they had named Jane. Her purring had a strangely
tranquilizing effect, and he felt at peace. He was watching the
floating rectangle of the portal, which had steadily but slowly
descended over the last few hours. It was now only about seven feet
off the ground.

"If I could chin myself, I could get up there," he said. "But I
know I can't chin myself."

"Don't worry, it'll come down," Deena said.

They waited while the sun inched down the sky and a cool
breeze came up out of the forest. The other animals lazed in the
grass, some sleeping, others giving themselves tongue baths or

simply staring off, preoccupied with quiet thoughts. That these creatures were intelligent was very apparent. Once he and Deena had gotten over their initial fright, it had also been obvious that these strange animals could communicate emotions via some sort of telepathy.

Barnaby wondered about them. Were they truly intelligent, or simply emotionally sensitive and empathetic? Their life seemed a bit too idyllic to require much problem solving. He did a mental shrug. The jury was still out on dolphins and whales; who knew about these strange and marvelous creatures?

He checked the aperture once more. Still descending with clocklike slowness. He shaded his eyes. No, it had stopped. Or had it? It was difficult to tell. As long as it wasn't rising. Then again, a stay here might not be too bad. He wondered what it would be like. Were these animals carnivorous? They looked the part. He couldn't imagine them grazing and chewing cud. But they didn't seem aggressive enough to be killers.

Life might be pretty nice here. It was warm and sunny and quiet. He rather liked the place even though he didn't know much about it. He was very tired, and he needed a rest. The castle was simply too much for him. He had to find a place where there was no noise and no fighting and no huge white beasts with claws, no strange blue monsters. Just a nice quiet place where he could relax and not have to worry about . . . whatever. About getting back home. About castles and kings and knights of the Round Table and everyone running around like characters in an old Errol Flynn movie. Worse. None of it was real, of course. Couldn't be. It had to be a dream, had to be. Just a dream, and soon he'd wake up and he'd be back in familiar surroundings and everything would be fine. The world would be right again, no more nightmare, no more . . . dream. . . .

"Barnaby, wake up!"

"Huh?"

Barnaby sat up. Jane got to her feet and stared into the forest.

Deena pointed. "Somethin's going on over there. I smell smoke."

So did Barnaby. "How long was I asleep?"

"I dunno. I was asleep myself. Look."

A pall of gray smoke drifted above the trees, and the smell of burning wood came out of the forest on a hot, acrid wind.

"Forest fire!" Barnaby gasped. He turned and searched for the aperture. To his dismay, he found that it had risen to about ten feet. "Oh, no. My God, what'll we do?"

"We either get up to that window or run."

"I'll never make it, Deena."

"Neither will I. It's too high to jump up."

"Climb up on my shoulders."

"Okay, say I make it. What then?"

"Look for something up there. A rope, whatever you can find. We'll never outrun that fire. Come on. Alley-oop, and all that."

After some initial tries, Deena managed to climb and perch on Barnaby's shoulders. Shakily she tried to rise to a stand, but couldn't get purchase on Barnaby's sloping shoulders. He helped as best he could, letting her use his hands as supports. She tried again, slid off, and went tumbling in the grass.

All the animals had left the clearing except Jane and Buster, who stood looking on curiously, occasionally glancing back toward the rapidly approaching fire front. Streamers of thick black smoke now trailed through the clearing.

"That fire is racing a mile a minute," Barnaby said worriedly as the roar and crackle of flames came to his ears.

Deena mounted again, circus style, stepping up on Barnaby's angled thigh and leaping to a stand in one clean motion—but she lost her balance and fell again. It was the right approach, however, and they tried again. This time it worked, and Deena managed to balance herself precariously on Barnaby's shoulders.

"I got it!" she yelled as she hooked her fingers over the lower rim of the portal. "Push me up!"

"I . . . I can't—" Barnaby felt her weight come off his shoulders. He jammed the heel of his hand under her right shoe and lifted, then did the same with the left. He looked up and was struck by what would have been, to someone just arriving on the scene, the bewildering sight of a young black woman hanging on to a hole in the middle of the air. Grunting and puffing, Barnaby boosted her up as far as he could. Deena tried chinning herself, but her strength was not up to it. Her legs flailed out uselessly, with nothing to push against but air.

"I can't do it!" she cried.

"Yes, you can!" Barnaby glanced toward the source of the eye-searing smoke that now began to engulf the clearing. He could see flames quite clearly now as they licked at the underbrush and raved in the treetops. He looked up at Deena again. "Swing your leg up!"

Deena swung from side to side to get momentum, then kicked out with her right leg. The heel of her shoe caught the outside lip of the aperture, but slipped off, and she very nearly lost her tenuous finger-grip. She tried again with the left, to no avail. Then she got an idea and began to swing back and forth through the plane of the window, as if on a parallel bar. She increased the arc of her swing, then tucked her legs in and let the sudden increase in angular momentum boost her to chinning level. Her right leg shot up over the windowsill.

"You got it!" Barnaby shouted. "Get your arm over!"

Deena got more leg inside the window until she hung almost upside down. Using her legs more than her arms, she pulled herself up to where she could hook her right arm over the sill.

Barnaby watched her disappear inside the portal. Then Deena showed her head.

"I made it!" she cried. "Now what?"

"Is there anything up there we could use?"

"There ain't nothin'! No rope, no nothin'. Not even any furniture. Oh, Barnaby, I'm sorry."

"Yeah," Barnaby said, turning to watch tongues of flame ignite the dry grass at the edge of the clearing.

"I'm gonna go get help," Deena yelled. "Maybe I can find a rope."

"Forget it!" Barnaby told her. "There isn't time. I gotta make a run for it. I—"

He looked down. Jane was nuzzling the backs of his knees. Buster had something clenched between his teeth. It was one chewed end of a very long and very thick vine.

"Thank you," Barnaby said in astonishment. He took the vine. It seemed long enough and strong enough. But now the problem was one of Deena's ability to haul him up. He didn't see how she could do it.

"Throw it up!" Deena yelled.

Barnaby took the vine in both hands and tested its strength. It had a tough, spiral structure that made it almost as strong as top-grade hemp. Barnaby coiled the vine—there was about twenty feet of it—and tossed it up through the aperture. Soon one end came trailing down.

"Tie it good!" she called.

"You'll never be able to lift me!"

"I got help!"

Barnaby looped the vine around his middle and tied what he hoped was a nonslip knot. "Ready!" he shouted.

Slowly he rose. When he was high enough, he reached up and threw both arms over the sill and pulled with all his might. Two sets of arms grabbed him and hauled him up and through the portal. He tumbled to the floor and lay still, gasping and wheezing.

Having caught his breath, he sat up. Deena and a stranger were smiling at him. The man was dark-haired and bearded, wearing a green doublet and jerkin, green hose, and thigh-high boots of soft buff leather. A saber in a gilded scabbard hung at his side.

"Thank you," Barnaby said to the man.

"'Twas nothing." The man peered out the portal, through which smoke drifted.

Barnaby got up and looked out. Buster and Jane had reached the far end of the clearing. They stopped and took one last look back at the portal.

Goodbye, new friends.

Barnaby heard them as if they had shouted it. He waved, watching the two beautiful animals disappear into the brush.

A moment later, the clearing went up in an incandescent flash and they had to step back from the window.

"I owe you my life," Barnaby said. "My name's Barnaby Walsh."

The man took his hand.

"Kwip's the name," the green-clad, dark-bearded stranger said.

ELSEWHEN

THE RUINS LOOKED Mayan only because of the jungle setting, but the architecture was just as strange, the carved glyphs just as enigmatic, the hidden crypts as dark and foreboding. Froglike inhuman faces stared out in bas-relief from the walls of buildings whose functions were difficult to guess. They could have been temples, or just as easily dormitories or warehouses. Inside, bare rooms were laid out in bewildering mazes. In one of the larger buildings there was a spacious, rotundalike chamber which did evoke a religious atmosphere, and it was there that the foursome stopped to rest after touring the ruins. The heat was awful, the jungle air a sodden, mist-hung pall that shrouded everything, stifling and oppressing.

The interior walls of the "temple" were profusely decorated in enigmatic frescolike paintings.

"Real interesting," Gene remarked sarcastically, dabbing at his forehead with his undertunic, which he had doffed, along with his cuirass, in the heat.

"I think so," Linda said, examining a curious mural which depicted strange bipedal beings doing even stranger things. She couldn't quite make sense of it.

"Well, I wanted civilization," Gene said, stalking around the huge polygonal room. "I didn't count on a dead one, though."

"No," Linda said, "I guess there's no chance of finding a super-weapon here."

"A knife, maybe, good for cutting out the hearts of sacrificial victims."

"Yuck."

"Don't worry. If they indulged in that sort of thing, they're long dead."

Snowclaw said, *"Ghallarst miggan."*

"I was wondering how it was affecting you," Gene said, walking over to his white-furred friend.

Snowclaw sat down wearily on a stone bench and let his sword clatter to the floor. *"Hallahust ullum nogakk, tuir ullum miggast kwahnahg."*

"Don't die on us, Snowy," Gene said, laying a hand on Snowclaw's snout and turning his head a bit. "Your eyes do look glazed."

"How can you understand what he's saying?" Sheila asked.

"I don't, not really," Gene said. "But you can get the general drift. I've been listening to his jabber for almost a year now, while at the same time listening to a simultaneous translation. You get to the point where the jabber becomes semi-intelligible."

"That's amazing," Sheila said. "Back in the castle I could understand Snowy perfectly, even though I knew he was doing a lot of barking and growling. But now it sounds just like a lot of barking and growling."

"Yeah, I know what you mean. It took me a long time before I could understand him at all this way."

"But I still don't see how."

"Well, I heard somebody say once that if you watched enough foreign movies with subtitles, you'd eventually learn the languages. I never believed it, but it seems to be true. Either that or it's some kind of holdover effect of the castle's magic. I really don't know."

"What's Snowy saying?"

"He says he can't stand the heat, and that he has to cool off somehow, and soon, or he'll get really sick. He may even die."

"Oh, no."

"Yeah, it's going to be a problem."

"Hallosk ullum banthahlk nak gethakk."

Gene answered, "Sorry, chum. I wish there was something I could do."

Snowclaw said something else, and Gene nodded.

"What did he say?" Sheila asked.

"He said he'd be okay, but not to count on him in a fight. He's not feeling up to snuff."

"Poor baby." Sheila went over to Snowclaw and stroked the top of his massive head. Snowy encircled her waist with a sinewy arm and squeezed gently.

"Well, wonderful," Gene declared. "Here we are, stuck somewhere in the goddamn eightieth dimension. Just our luck. We had our choice of worlds—universes, for Christ's sake! What do we do? We pick some wild, jerkwater aspect that appears in the castle every two hundred years, or something. We buy ourselves a one-way ticket to Rod Serling's game room, that's what we do."

"It won't do any good to complain," Linda said.

"Do you mind if I complain just a little bit?"

"Be my guest," Linda answered with a shrug.

Gene stared at the floor awhile, then said, "I'm sorry, Linda. You're right."

"Forget it, Gene. There really isn't much we can do."

"What we have to do is some thinking." Gene plopped down on the edge of a circular stone platform that could have been an altar, or perhaps a stage or dais. "Thing is, I don't have a thought in my head. How do we go about chasing down a portal that could appear anywhere in this world, if it ever appears again?"

"It may crop up somewhere near," Linda said. "We just have to keep a sharp eye out for it."

"Our chances are pretty slim, Linda. We might just have to face that."

Linda looked away, her face set grimly. "I'm not sure I can. I don't have any magic here. I'm back to being what I was back home. Sort of a nothing."

"Linda, don't say that."

"It's true."

Gene frowned reproachfully. "You're not being fair to yourself."

"Please don't lecture me."

"I'm sorry." Gene wrung his hands for a while, clenching his jaw muscles. Then he stopped. "Did you actually try your magic?"

Linda was staring off. She came out of her reverie and said, "Huh?"

"I said, did you try your magic here?"

"First thing. I got all kinds of weird feelings, but nothing materialized. How about you?"

"I don't think I'll be able to tell for sure until I get into some sort of combat situation, but I suspect I am no longer ze greatest sword een France . . . or anywhere else, for that matter."

Linda looked off again, head cocked to one side, as if hearing something in the distance. Her eyes narrowed. "Something tells me there is magic here, somewhere."

"I sort of get that feeling, too," Gene said.

"But it's a different sort of magic. Very different. Not like the castle's."

"Yeah. Lot of help to us."

Brow furrowed, Linda fell into deep thought.

Sheila said, "Something tells me you guys will work it all out." She smiled wanly and gave a helpless shrug. "You guys are magicians. You can do anything. I've *seen* you do absolutely mind-boggling things, things that nobody would ever believe. And you did them as easy as falling out of bed!"

"Yeah, but that was back in the castle . . ." Gene broke off, something catching his eye across the room. He jumped up, crossed to the far wall, and stood with hands on hips, casting a critical eye over the strange mural. Moving nearer, he scrutinized several details, then stepped back again to take in the entire scene.

"There's something here," Linda said, slowly looking around the great chamber. "In this room." She stared curiously at the circular platform.

Sheila got up and walked to Gene's side.

"What does that look like to you?" Gene asked her, pointing to the middle of the painting.

"Where, there?"

"Yeah, that rectangle near where the thing with all the teeth is. Behind it."

"Yuck, what is that?"

"That's what I'm asking you."

"No, I mean the thing with all the teeth. What a horrible-looking thing."

"Some kind of demon or monster. And I think it's guarding that rectangle."

"What rectangle?"

"Well, it's hard to see with all the gingerbread. I missed it at first. Sort of ignore all that rococo stuff around it and inside it. See that box?''

"Oh, okay. Yeah, now I see it. Could it be . . . ''

"Yep, I think that's the portal. And I think this place was a temple for the cult that worshipped it. Or whatever they did. It stands to reason that strange, inexplicable holes in the air would wind up being thought of as miraculous things. Doorways to the realm of the gods, whatever.''

"Yeah, it stands to reason, all right. But what does the painting mean?''

Gene lifted his damp shoulders. "Who knows?''

Linda called, "Gene?''

Sheila and Gene walked back to the stone altar. Linda was standing in the middle of it.

"I feel something here,'' she said. "There's some kind of force, some kind of . . . *thing* going on here.''

Gene turned around and looked back at the painting. "Hey, that's it! It's gotta be!''

"What is it?'' Linda said.

"The portal materializes here,'' Gene said, pointing to the middle of the altar. "Look at the painting, underneath the rectangle. A circle. It's gotta be this thing we're standing on.''

"That must be it!'' Sheila jumped once and clapped her hands.

"If they built a temple around this spot,'' Gene went on, "it must mean that the portal appears here every so often.'' He sighed. "Of course, the question is *how* often. Every hour? Every other Tuesday? Once a year? Or maybe once a millennium.''

They surveyed the room, looking at the other wall paintings. All were just as enigmatic as the one with the portal, if not more so.

"It'd take a team of archeologists to make any sense of this stuff,'' Gene said cheerlessly. "All the answers are written all over the damn walls, if only we could read them.''

Linda said, "I guess the only answer is that we have to wait. Wait for the portal to appear.''

Pennsylvania Turnpike, Near Bedford

"You up?" Trent asked.

Incarnadine touched the control button, and the leather bucket seat tilted up. "I am now." He rubbed his eyes. "What's that infernal buzzing?"

"Just a danger signal."

"Oh." Incarnadine looked back through the rear window. "Nothing but a trailer truck, it looks like, back about half a mile."

"That must be it. We're coming to a three-mile downgrade. If he's going to make his move, it'll be when we're going down this mountain."

"You seem fairly sure. It could just be a trailer truck."

Trent shook his head. "My spells rarely fail me. Get that gun out and get ready."

"Will do."

Trent increased speed. The cold rural night howled by, whistling through the car's air vents and a hairline fresh-air crack that Incarnadine had left between the window glass and the weather stripping on the door on his side.

A pair of bright headlights grew in the rear window. Trent's eyes shifted between the road and the rearview mirror. Incarnadine watched out of the mirror on his side. The truck drew up to the Mercedes, headlights glaring, its huge engine revved to a frenzy. It hung there a moment, then suddenly swerved into the passing lane. It went thundering by, plunging down the steep hill, a leviathan of the night, its flanks glittering with dozens of tiny red and yellow lights.

"What was that about fail-safe spells?"

Trent seemed discomfited. "Something may be up ahead, waiting for us. The car we saw back at the Burger King, maybe."

They drove on for several uneventful minutes. The road was dark in both directions.

"Are you sure your Earth magic is all it's cracked up to be?" Incarnadine asked.

Trent gave his head a quick shake. "Can't figure it."

Like the sudden deadly blooming of a nuclear fireball, the crest of the hill behind them lit up in a blaze of light. Something big topped the rise and rolled down the hill, approaching with unbelievable speed.

"I take it back," Incarnadine said. "Your lookout spell isn't fooling."

"Interesting," Trent observed. "What do you make of it?"

"Not your average tractor-semitrailer."

The thing behind them was twice as big as any conventional vehicle, its array of headlights like a blinding galaxy of suns. The windshield and windows glowed strangely blue, and yellow flames shot out of twin exhaust stacks at either side of the cab. Swooping down the hill at breakneck speed, the spectral truck howled like a psychotic beast chained in the fires of Hell.

Trent floored the accelerator and wheeled the Mercedes around a bend to the right as the road continued down the side of the mountain. The speedometer crept past 80 mph, edging into the red.

"Got your seat belt on?" Trent asked casually.

"When did they start putting these things in automobiles?"

Trent didn't answer as he mashed the accelerator into the floorboard. The thing behind them was still gaining.

"We'll never outrun it," Incarnadine said.

"You're right. I wonder if he means to crowd us off the road, or simply run over us."

"It looks quite capable of either tactic."

"Inky?"

"Yes, Trent?"

"I think we've had it."

The monster vehicle closed steadily. Trent began swerving between lanes, and the demonic semi followed suit. There was very little room for maneuvering; the right shoulder was narrow, edging an almost vertical wall of blasted rock. An aluminum barrier ran between the roadways. There was no emergency lane and no place to pull off.

Ghastly blue light flooded the interior of the Mercedes as the truck drew close. An ear-splitting horn blast rent the night, and gouts of flame belched from the twin exhaust stacks. The truck's contoured windshield looked like a phantasmal roaming eye, radiating otherworldly light. The truck tried to pass, and Trent blocked its path, eliciting another angry blast of the demonic horn. Incarnadine thought his ears would burst. The truck swerved right, and Trent dodged back into the right lane.

"Watch it," Incarnadine said.

"I can't let it get abreast of us."

The truck stopped weaving and crept closer to the rear of the Mercedes.

"You can't let it—" Incarnadine began to say.

The truck bumped into the rear of the Mercedes and backed off; then, engine yowling, it sprang forward and slammed into the car, its huge burnished grille looking like a shark's mouth, huge and hungry and slavering for the kill.

Another impact came, and the Mercedes began to fishtail. Trent countersteered and straightened out. Again, the demon semi lunged forward, but this time Trent whipped extra power out of the car's already overtaxed engine and pulled away.

"Steer for me, Inky!" Trent shouted. "I have to have my arms free!"

Incarnadine leaned over and grabbed the wheel with both hands. The car swerved just as he took control, and he fought to bring it back into line. At his left ear he heard Trent chanting a complex and mostly unintelligible incantation. Trent's fingers worked off to either side, moving in precise patterns.

The road underwent a sudden and quite unexplainable transformation. It changed color, from murky, half-seen gray to bright yellow. It also widened considerably, somehow acquiring a multi-colored canopy like the roof of a tunnel. Streamers of color flowed past, along with geometrical shapes and strange designs.

Trent laughed triumphantly, taking back the steering wheel. "Shades of Stanley Kubrick!"

"Who?"

Incarnadine craned his neck and looked out the rear window. The truck was still tailing but had dropped back. As he watched, it continued to fall behind. Wherever the Mercedes was going, the truck either could not or did not want to follow.

Incarnadine looked ahead and whistled his admiration. "Neat trick, little brother. What do you call this?"

Trent flipped a palm over. "A shortcut. The tricky part is getting back to normal reality."

"Are we ready to do that yet?"

"Not quite. Enjoy the show."

Incarnadine sat back and watched the play of light, color, and pattern. Brilliant shapes raced out at them from an incandescent night, flowing past with ever-increasing speed. There was no longer a road now, just a long tunnel of reticulated luminescence. At its distant vanishing point, somewhere out near infinity where all the glowing lines converged, a brilliant starburst of light coalesced. It grew and increased in intensity. Incarnadine got the impression that it was getting closer.

"See that light?"

"Yes," Incarnadine said. "What is it?"

"I've never driven long enough to find out. Want to?"

"I would, under other circumstances."

"Right. Where's the demonic eighteen-wheeler?"

Incarnadine looked. "Nowhere in sight."

"Okay, hang on."

The tunnel of light faded gradually until at last the mundane turnpike again rolled under the wheels of the Mercedes. The terrain had flattened out somewhat. Clearly they were on a different section of the road.

"Good job, Trent. I liked your shortcut."

"And here's the exit. State Route 711, right?"

"I'm not sure I like the numerological implications."

Trent turned off the highway, gradually slowing on the long, curving exit ramp. The toll booths lay up ahead, on the other side of the overpass.

"There it is," Trent said, looking to the left.

The monster semi rolled by on the highway beneath, screeching its frustration. Incarnadine watched it come out the other side of the underpass and go hurtling down the road, a shiny black juggernaut trimmed in glistening chrome.

It rolled about a thousand feet down the turnpike before vanishing in a burst of crimson flame.

KEEP—FAMILY RESIDENCE

THE ROOM WAS full of antique furniture representative of many periods. On the walls hung ancient tapestries depicting stag hunts, tournaments, battles, and other manly pastimes. Many a quaint and curious artifact lay about: there were weapons, articles of military apparel, inscribed drinking cups, medallions, and other mementos, all prominently displayed in glass-fronted cabinets.

Ferne stood in the middle of the room at a table, upon which sat a most extraordinary device. It was large, taking up most of the tabletop, and in the main consisted of porcelain cylinders, glass spheres, copper tubes, and other less readily identifiable components. A small plate of frosted glass rose from the works inside a copper frame. The device was in operation. Blue sparks crackled within the glass spheres, and faint multicolored aureoles enveloped a few of the other components. The glass plate glowed with a milky light.

Ferne was bent over the device, twisting dials and knobs on a control panel. She studied a quartz gauge, noting the fluctuations of the small needle within. She adjusted a control until the needle stabilized, then threw a toggle switch.

The screen came to life with the images of three individuals sitting behind a long narrow table. They appeared human, and wore gray suitcoats over black turtlenecks. Their faces were pale and thin, and their eyes were cold, hard, and black. Short dark hair grew above their high foreheads.

"Your Royal Highness!" the middle individual beamed, smiling. "So nice of you to visit us."

"I am pleased to see you all," Ferne said. "May I sit down?"

"By all means, Your Highness. In fact, we beg your forgiveness for sitting in your presence, but we didn't—"

"You needn't apologize," she said, sitting down. "You doubtless know that this device merely projects my image."

"Of course. But it has been quite some time since anyone communicated with us in this manner."

"Quite so. I can't speak for my family, but know I haven't used the Universal Projector since I was a youngster."

"We remember. A most curious device."

"Yes. My ancestors mainly used it to bring wayward vassals into line. A sudden apparition in the night was usually enough to reduce any strong-willed underling to a compliant mass of jelly."

"One can well imagine. But why rely on a mechanical contrivance to effect such a purpose?"

"The device is not quite mechanical. It works by tapping interuniversal forces, which, as you know, are the source of all magical energy. But it makes unnecessary all the usual appurtenances and folderol—talismans, chanting, gestures, and the like. Long-distance image projection requires subtle spellcasting. This instrument facilitates the process greatly. The device is quite ancient, though, and is somewhat crude. But it does work."

The middle one smiled warmly. "In any event, we are always glad to talk with you, regardless of the means used."

"Thank you. May we now proceed to the main order of business?"

"Certainly."

"I assume you received my last communication."

The one on the left spoke. "Yes, Your Royal Highness. We have given your proposal a great deal of study."

"And?"

The individual on the right answered. "We find much of merit. We regret to say, however, that the terms are not entirely satisfactory."

Ferne's dark eyebrows curled down. "If I may ask, what specifically is not to your liking?"

"Well, there are a number of specific issues," the middle one said. "But we think it safe to say that the question of sharing power is the main stumbling block."

"Ah." Ferne nodded. "I had a feeling it would be."

The one on the right said, "Generally speaking, we do not feel that the rewards specified are commensurate with services rendered."

"You want more worlds under your exclusive control."

"Actually," the middle one said apologetically, "to be very blunt about it, we think that your offer was totally inadequate. Of course, we would be willing to negotiate on the final number, but we were thinking orders of magnitude higher."

"No doubt," Ferne said. "But I am afraid I can't budge from the terms of my offer. There is only so much power I'm willing to relinquish."

"But there are so many worlds. Surely you can't be thinking of administrating them all on your own."

"Of course not," Ferne said. "Not even a tenth part of them, nor a hundredth. My imperial ambitions are quite limited. This sharply distinguishes me from my brother, who has never had any imperial ambitions at all. I think him absurd. Surely an instrument such as Castle Perilous deserves better use than to serve as a hostel for vagabonds and beggars. Hardly fitting for what may be the most powerful artifact in the whole of Creation."

"We quite agree," the individual on the left said. "That is why we feel that such a resource must be shared. This has long been a bone of contention between your family and us. As for ourselves, of course, we have no 'imperial ambitions,' as you put it. We seek only to impose a benevolent order. The state of the universes is chaotic in the extreme. We merely wish to establish a semblance of rationality."

"Oh, I quite agree with those sentiments," Ferne said. "The universes are in a dreadful mess, and so is the castle. And the unfathomable thing about it is that this has been the case ever since the castle came to be! Apparently the will to power runs weak in my family."

"We would not agree. Your family has jealously guarded its power, and its secrets, for generations."

"Guarded its power, yes," Ferne said. "Maintained it, yes. But used it? No. Absolutely not. What I seek to establish is merely a measure of . . . well, of *intestinal fortitude*. And it's high time someone tried."

"We seem to agree on a few general principles, at least," the middle individual said. "Surely this can provide a basis for working out our differences."

"Perhaps, but time is running short. The invaders will very soon consolidate their hold on the castle."

With a casual shrug the one on the left said, "From your description of them, we don't think they will be much trouble."

"Do not underestimate them."

"We believe we haven't, Your Royal Highness."

"Very well," Ferne said. "You are the best judge of your abilities. And I am quite sure they are considerable. Also, do not underestimate me. I am fully aware that there is a good deal that remains unspoken between us."

The three individuals exchanged glances. "Such as?" the middle one asked.

"Many things. True intentions, motivations. Desires and goals. Also circumstances. For instance, I am aware that what I am seeing now is not your true appearance. I have also gotten the impression in my dealings with you that your world or your society is not composed of individuals, but is in reality a single mass entity of some sort. I am not sure of this, but it remains a possibility in my mind. I remember asking you about this very point long ago. Whenever I pressed for an answer, I got only evasions."

"There is of course a perfectly logical explanation for many of your doubts and reservations," the one on the right said. "Our universes differ widely in many respects. In fact, the differences are profound enough to greatly hamper mutual understanding."

"Doubtless so. I'm sure a mere mortal could never understand beings such as you."

"Forgive our saying this, but your terminology is somewhat inappropriate."

"Is it? Only you would know. But let us return to concretes. In return for the privileges I have accorded you, you will aid my brother Deems and me in our fight to take back our family stronghold from the invaders who have usurped it. If we are successful, I am willing to provide you with exclusive access to a few hundred universes of your choice. You will be free to do what you want with them. That is the sum and substance of my proposal. Do you accept or not?"

"In principle, yes," the middle individual said. "However—"

"That is all I am willing to offer. I am afraid I am not disposed to negotiate any further."

The three were silent for a moment. Then the individual in the middle said, "We will have to confer and give you our answer at a later date."

"I want it in an hour."

"We need time to—"

"I want your answer in an hour," she said tightly.

There was a pause. Then: "As you wish."

"I will call you."

She flipped the toggle, and the images faded. With some effort, she rose from the chair.

The far door opened and Deems came in.

"Did you communicate with them?" he asked, walking over.

"Yes," she said.

"Are you ill? You look peaked. Let me get you some refreshment."

"Thank you. Negotiating with them is draining. Don't you remember how it was?"

Deems went to a small cabinet and took out a bottle of sherry and two glasses. He filled both glasses and gave one to Ferne, who had seated herself on a recliner. "We all toyed with the Hosts of Hell at one time or another. Fascinating lot. Hideously dangerous, of course, which made them all the more alluring to the young and disgruntled. Yes, I well remember their incessant attempts to seduce one of us into letting them out of their hellhole." Deems sighed disconsolately. "And I suppose they've finally succeeded."

"Had they accomplished it when we were children, they would have overrun the castle."

"And would have taken control of Creation."

"Perhaps, although I think it's possible to overestimate them. They are powerful, but surely not godlike."

"Be that as it may, I hope you and Inky can control them, as you claim you can. There'll be hell to pay—quite literally, I should imagine!—if you're mistaken."

"You worry too much, Deems. You always did."

"What if Inky doesn't give in? Do you really need him?"

"No, not really. I think I have a few things over on Inky these days. Though his cooperation would make things a little easier, I admit."

Deems looked at her askance. "Why do I have trouble believing you?"

She laughed. "Don't be silly. I've told you everything. You have no reason to doubt me. Besides, what do you care about all this? You'll get your gold, one way or another."

Chewing his lip and looking dissatisfied, Deems sat down on an ancient thronelike chair and threw one chain-mailed leg up over the armrest. "Don't think I don't care about Perilous."

She laughed scornfully. "Deems, you've never cared for anything but drinking, wenching, and the occasional brawl."

"I don't deny that, but it doesn't mean I'd suffer lightly the destruction of my family's ancestral home."

"There won't be any destruction, Deems. Not unless Inky chooses to detransmogrify the castle."

Deems sat up. "Gods. Do you think he would?"

"Undoing the spell that maintains the castle and then immediately recasting the spell would be the optimum solution for him. In the process, everything and everyone in the place would . . . well, *vanish* for want of a better word. No one really knows what happens. In any event, it would be a new shuffle of the deck. Recast the spell, transform the demon back into a castle, and everything reverts to what it was before any of this started." She took a sip of wine. "Of course, there is one problem. All of that is vastly more easy to say than to do. He was lucky once, a year or so ago. I don't think he'd risk it again. He'll see the wisdom of compromise. Eventually."

"You must open the gateway for him."

"No! Let him stew a while longer yet. We have to convince him we mean business."

"What if he breaks through on his own?"

"If he does, we take him into custody. It's that simple."

"Nothing is simple with old Inky, Ferne. You ought to know that."

"Oh, I know. I know."

Deems sat back and stared moodily into his glass. "If you would have suggested to me that we would have to deal with the Hosts, I would never have gone along with this. I would have taken Inky's side—gold or no gold—and would have fought you tooth and nail."

"I realize that," she said. "But that's not what happened. Is it?"

Deems fell silent for a long spell. Then he took a deep breath. "Damn me." He drained his glass in one gulp. "I've been a bloody fool."

"It's a little too late to back out, Deems dear."

"I've got to talk to Inky."

"No! You can't reach him."

"The Projector."

"I wouldn't advise it."

"Advise me no advice, woman." He rose, crossed to the table that held the Projector, and began fiddling with the device's control panel.

"Deems, Deems," she said in mock lament. "The Projector merely channels a spell and gives it form. The operator has to provide the mental energy."

"I know there's a simple spell that sets up the device. Then it's merely a matter of calibrating—"

"Yes, you can find a book of standard utility spells—in the library. Your problem is fighting your way through hordes of invaders to get there."

Deems stopped fiddling and thrust his fists against his hips, glaring at his sister. "Damned meddling bitch!"

"How *dare* you speak that way to me."

"I'll speak any way I bloody well—" He broke off. Brow lowered, Deems eyed her as if seeing both her and the situation anew. "You never meant to bargain with Inky, did you? You want to keep him out of the castle. Do away with him entirely, if you have to. Isn't that true?"

Ferne settled back in the recliner and lifted the glass to her lips. "And if it is?" she said quietly.

"But . . ." He threw out his arms helplessly. "But you can't hope to prevail against the Hosts by yourself! Surely you don't think yourself the equal of Inky as a magician. No one is. He's the master of Perilous! Only he can tap the castle's deepest source of power."

"Because he's a man?"

Deems was brought up short. "Eh? Because he's a—? Well . . . yes!" He shrugged expansively. "I *suppose*."

"You suppose."

"This is ridiculous! Females may succeed to the throne only in the absence of a suitable male heir apparent. You know that as well as I do. What of it?"

"That is the tradition. But it has no bearing on who may tap the castle's power. You silly men have simply got to realize—"

Deems silenced her with an upraised hand. "Stop confusing the issue! I see now what you've done, and why you did it. This was all a scheme to divide the family, clearing the way for your bid to power. You haven't the least intention of sharing power—with Inky, or me, or anyone else! You want all of it!"

"I deserve it," she said. "I'm the only one who's not afraid to use it."

"But surely you realize that the Hosts don't mean to share with you, either!"

"I don't know about that. They have certain ambitions, but they can be placated for the time being. Pacified."

"Appeased, you mean?"

Ferne's blue eyes turned to ice. "I needed allies, powerful allies! Who was I to turn to? You? Trent? Or maybe my fat cow of a sister."

Deems grunted. "Dorcas is the best one of a bad litter."

"Pig shit. I needed allies, and I found them."

"Not yet. Not while they're still ensconced in their hellhole." She laughed, throwing her head back.

Appalled, Deems regarded her. "What in the name of all the gods . . ." Understanding bloomed on his face. Paling, he brought his hand to his throat. "The gods be merciful. Woman, tell me you haven't already unbuttoned them."

She continued laughing and he knew.

Ashen-faced, he sat down and stared at the floor. When he spoke, his voice was empty. "Inky's the only card you hold. He's the threat you're holding over them. The threat that Inky will return and detransmogrify the castle."

"And I have him bottled up," she said, still giggling. "Corked." She burst into another bout of laughter.

"It was the security spell on the Hosts' portal that you undid first," Deems droned on. "One of the oldest in the castle. One of Ervoldt's spells. No wonder Inky was concerned. No wonder he raced off to earth to find Trent. Trent specialized in ancient magic. Inky probably needed his advice. Doubtless Inky suspected Trent of having done it, but in any event he had to confront him."

Recovered from her mirth, Ferne regarded her brother with raised eyebrows. "Deems, this new pastime of yours may prove your undoing."

"Eh?"

"Thinking. You've done so little of it in your life. This much exertion all at once . . . Well, it can't be healthy." She took another sip. "Anyway, you're wrong in all the details. Details are important, Deems."

Deems slowly rose and crossed to the liquor cabinet. He poured himself another glass of sherry, retired to the leather throne again, and sank into it.

Suddenly he bolted upright and set his glass down on a side table. He fixed his sister in a penetrating stare. "Here's more thinking for you. If the Hosts have had access to the castle for—how long?—six months? If they've had time to send out scouts, or agents, or whatever, may they not now be on Earth trying to do Inky in?"

"I doubt it."

"You doubt it? Great gods, woman! You mean to say the possibility exists?"

"Well, yes. Before I stabilized the Earth portal, it was free for anyone to use, if it could be located. But why would the Hosts send agents to Earth?"

"To keep an eye on you, of course! Tell me, are any of your servants at your Earth residence?"

"Of course, some of my bodyguards. Their job is to keep Inky from—"

"Listen to me. Have you hired any new servants within the last six months?"

She thought. "Yes. Those bodyguards, in fact." Suddenly Ferne became motionless, a strange light in her eyes. She stared off for a moment. Then she shrugged, and drank the last of the sherry. "I suppose the possibility *does* exist." Smiling sweetly, she held out her glass. "Do be a dear and fetch me more wine."

TEMPLE

"TRY IT AGAIN," Gene said.

Linda put out her hands and closed her eyes. A china plate with a hamburger on it materialized on the stone floor of the temple.

Gene picked the hamburger up and bit into it, tasting it clinically. "Better than the last one," he pronounced. "Edible, but still not what you'd call gourmet."

"It's getting a little easier," Linda said. "But I doubt if I'll ever be as good as I was in the castle."

"Well, that goes without saying. The castle is a huge power source."

Sheila said, "Let me see if I understand this. You're saying that this world is one in which magic works. Right?"

"Right," Gene said.

"But it's not the same kind of magic that's in the castle?"

"Right again. Different universe, different laws."

"But you say you're slowly getting used to this different kind of magic."

Linda answered, "Sort of. But, again, it's not going to be the same as back in the castle. Everything is *real* easy there. Maybe too easy. We got spoiled."

"At least we won't starve," Gene said, holding up the half-eaten hamburger. Then he looked over at Snowclaw, who was sleeping on the narrow stone bench near the wall. "But that doesn't solve all our problems."

"It doesn't solve any of them," Linda said. "We can't stay here."

"Right," Gene said. "So, I say we try it."

"I'm not up to it yet," Linda said. "If I can't conjure a hamburger right, how the heck could I do a portal?"

"Well, let's look at it this way. There are an infinite number of possible hamburgers. Now, an *haute cuisine,* gourmet, taste-treat kind of hamburger is going to be pretty hard to find out of all those others. But there's only one portal to the castle from this world. One. It shouldn't be hard for you to find it and fetch it here. You follow?"

Linda giggled. "Gene, you always have a strange way of looking at things. I don't think I find things and fetch them. I just whip 'em up and they appear."

"No, I think you *do* find things. How else can you explain your ability to conjure things you've never seen before? Like the first time you whipped up food for Snowy, food that you'd never imagined, let alone set eyes on. What I think you do is this. You send out feelers or sensors into interuniversal space and locate stuff. Then, somehow, you pull the stuff in."

Linda looked dubious. "How do I know where to find what I want?"

"I don't know. I'm not saying this is the actual way it happens. It's just one way to think about it. Skeptical-rationalist that I am, I can't bring myself to believe that you create something out of nothing. It must come from somewhere. There must be a law of conservation of . . . whatever. Mass, energy, you name it, even in magical universes. What you do is merely find stuff and transport it. It takes energy, and the castle supplies that. But the amount of energy you'd need to create something even as small as a quarter-pound hamburger would be stupendous! E equals MC squared—you know?"

"Yeah, I think I get you. But what's going to supply the power here?"

"This temple, maybe. You said you could feel it. It's a different kind of power. Think of it this way: the castle's AC, but this world is DC. Actually it's probably better to say that they're both AC, but not in phase—but forget that, forget that. Do you get the drift?"

"Gotcha," Linda said.

"I understand it," Sheila said. "I think you ought to go ahead and try, Linda."

"I'm game," Linda said.

Gene got up and searched the stone floor. "I saw some markings over here. Yeah, here's one of them. See this circle?"

"There's another over there," Linda said.

"Yeah, there are four of them, positioned around the altar. From what I can glean from the murals, four priests stood in those circles when they conjured the portal."

"If that's what they did."

Gene threw out his arms. "Hey, look. What do we have to lose?"

"Famous last words."

"It'll work, it's gotta. What I'm proposing is this. There are four of us. We each stand in one of these circles, and we all do our best to conjure together. It might work if we try to reproduce as many aspects of the conjuring ceremony as we can."

"Can't hurt."

"Wait a minute," Sheila said. "I hope you don't expect any magic from me. I know I don't have any."

"You never can tell," Gene said. "It usually sneaks up on you."

"Well, okay. It can't hurt."

"Yeah. You know, it is starting to sound like famous last words. But we gotta try it. Okay, everybody. Sheila, wake up Snowy, will you?"

Sheila did, and Snowy woke up with a start. Snarling, he lashed out with one arm. Sheila ducked, narrowly missing having her head taken off.

"Whew! Is he better after he's had his coffee?"

"Sorry, Sheila," Gene said. "He's suffering pretty bad in this heat."

"Oh, it's all right. He didn't mean it. Did you, Snowy?"

Snowclaw rubbed his eyes. He growled again, then groaned and got up.

"How are you feeling, big fella?" Gene asked.

Snowy made a gesture that said, *"So-so."*

As best he could, Gene tried to explain what they were about to do. Snowclaw seemed to understand.

They all took their positions. Silence fell in the temple. Outside, distant hooting calls echoed in the jungle, punctuating a wider, greater silence. Dripping water plop-plopped somewhere off in a dark corner of the ruined building.

Sheila felt a warm rivulet of sweat trickle down her back, but she didn't dare scratch. Everyone looked deadly serious, and she didn't want to break the mood. She remained skeptical about the whole enterprise, but did her best to concentrate, calling up images of the portals she had seen. There hadn't been very many, and there wasn't very much to visualize except for a hole in the air, which was a difficult concept to grasp, much less visualize. She tried thinking of the castle and how much she wished she were back there. Not because she liked the place, but because the castle seemed one step closer to the world she had lost.

But was that the way she really felt? Part of her wanted to go back home, but another part was curious about the castle itself. She had found new friends there, people who shared some of the same personal problems. Everyone had been friendly so far, for the most part. But that wasn't the entire explanation for her attraction to the place. Where else in the world—in the universe? (or universes?)—would one be likely to meet a wide variety of beings, intelligent beings, *who were not human*? She felt privileged, somehow, to have met Snowclaw. She hadn't seen many other nonhumans besides the Bluefaces, but she'd heard enough to have been struck by the wonder of it all.

Wonder. Yes, that was it. The place was *wonderful*, in the sense of being full of wondrous sights and things. It wasn't always wonderful in the colloquial sense—sometimes it was absolutely frightening and very unpleasant. But it was so totally different from her former existence. Life back home was boring, dreary, and full of small frustrations. And it wasn't entirely safe, either, what with wars, disasters, terrorism, crime, etc., etc., check any daily newspaper. So, what did her old life have to offer that her new life didn't? The food was better here, she had to admit that. Not here, in the temple, in whatever world this was, but in the castle, where she wanted to be now. She had to get back there, so that Gene and Snowy could beat the crap out of those blue guys and take the castle back—so Sheila could get something good to eat again! Yeah, she wanted to be back in the dining room with all that terrific food. Those blue guys sure were jerks! Spoiling everything—

"Forget it, Sheila," she heard Gene say.

"Huh?" She opened her eyes and looked around. Gene, Linda, and Snowy had left their stations and were walking toward her.

"Forget it," Gene said. "We'll try again. Maybe Linda needs to practice more."

Linda said, "Gene, look."

"What?"

They all beheld what had appeared at the center of the circular altar. Standing there was the upright oblong of the portal, dark castle stone visible on the other side.

"Let's go!" Gene yelled.

They ran through the portal in single file, Gene with sword drawn leading the way.

"Great White Stuff!" Snowy shouted as he came through. "I thought I was going to die in that heat!"

"You okay now?" Gene asked.

"Yeah, I'll be fine now. I'm never going to complain about this place again."

Linda was staring at Sheila. "You did it," she said.

"Me?" Sheila said. "How is that possible?"

"I don't know. I tried, and it didn't work. I couldn't summon the portal. You kept trying, and you did it."

"But—"

"Linda's right," Gene said. "It must have been your magic. How you got it in the temple is anybody's guess. But I'm guessing you had it here all the time and just didn't realize it."

Sheila lifted her shoulders. "Whatever you guys say. All I did is wish to be back here."

"Well, this is the only place I know of where wishes *are* horses and beggars go riding all over the goddamn place. You wished, and you got. Which brings up an interesting question."

Linda said, "Yeah! Maybe Sheila's talent is whipping up portals!"

Sheila said, "Huh?"

"Possibility," Gene said thoughtfully. He pointed to a blank wall. "Try to materialize a portal, say, right here."

"What portal?"

"Uh, well, let's go for the big money. The portal that leads back home."

Sheila's eyes widened. "Do you think that's possible?"

"Why not? Try it. Or any portal. Give it a go."

Sheila tried, but she just didn't know how to go about it.

"Something's wrong," she said. "Back in the temple it was different. Like you said, different universe, different laws. I can feel the magic *here,* though. Before, I don't think I did. Or at least I didn't know I was feeling it.''

Gene looked annoyed. "This is getting complicated. You can do it back there but not here. Linda's the other way around. Now *you* have to get used to the castle's laws. Hell, why isn't anything ever simple?'' He squared himself into a heroic stance. "Well, hell. Us John Wayne types ain't much for subtleties.''

"What happened to Cyrano?" Linda wanted to know.

"That big-nosed pansy, fighting with those skinny swords? Hmph!''

"Gene, I think you're the one who's suffering from the heat.''

"Hey, I'm hungry. How 'bout rustling up some grub, woman?''

"Right away, pardner.''

"Yeah, *Samantha*. Wiggle your nose, cutesylike, and bewitch us something to eat.''

"Okay, *Darin*.''

Snowclaw leaned toward Sheila and asked quietly, "Do all humans act silly like this a lot of the time?''

Sheila laughed. "Yeah.''

It was Linda who saw the bodies first. The group had been walking down the corridor, and she was first to turn the corner. She stopped dead and put her hand over her mouth. Gene drew his sword, came round the corner, and halted. Frowning, he slowly put his sword back in its scabbard.

Sheila peeked around the corner. The hallway ahead was littered with dead Bluefaces, dozens of them, most in a profound state of dismemberment. The sight didn't sicken her as much as it would have only the day before.

Gene examined a few of the corpses, then turned to his companions.

"Someone else is in the castle," he said.

KEEP—NEAR THE WELL TOWER

KWIP HAD BEEN a thief most of his life, having apprenticed himself as a youngster by stealing fruit from hucksters' wagons in Market Square, in the town of Dunwiddin, his home. He recalled many a merry chase through the streets, keeping a half-step ahead of the constable and his men. Hardly fond memories. The life of a thief was bleak indeed; and it had never been bleaker the night he had paced his cell waiting for the hangman's noose at dawn.

Bleak, dark night of the soul. Night, as well, of his liberation. For a miracle had occurred. The far wall of the cell had disappeared, become a doorway into a great castle, one such as he had never seen or even dreamed of.

Better yet, here in this grand and mysterious place he was free to pursue his occupation amazingly unhindered, so it would seem, by the authorities.

Which detracted from the fun somewhat, he had to admit.

But there was a catch. Aye, a pip of a one. There was nothing *in* the damnable place. There was not a garnet, not a fleck of amethyst, nor a gram of silver to be found in the entire castle, much less diamonds, rubies, or gold; leastwise, there was none he could discover. The blasted sconces were brass!

But the food was fit for princes, and it cost nothing for a man to eat his fill and drink himself to stupefaction. The Guests, by and rge, tended to be pleasant when they weren't minding their own business. Broadly speaking, the castle was a fine place in which to disport oneself.

If only he could find something worth stealing! Then the task would be to find a way back to his world. . . .

Ah, but then, he'd been over this same ground a thousand times since bumbling into the castle a year ago. There was no way back, or none easily found. And if he gave the matter enough thought, if he sat himself down and went about the task of sorting through his wishes, he usually found that he would as lief stay here. So be it.

Still, he hungered sore for some pastime to while away the hours, and questing for booty was as good as he could come up with. So it was his habit, at times, when the spirit moved him, to strike out into the far reaches of the castle in search of its fabled Treasure Room, which he had heard talk of. That such talk could be sheerest fancy, he well knew; but the quest was the thing. He needed it. It fortified him.

It was on such a trek that he had met the obese young man and his blackamoor mistress.

"You mean you ain't seen the Bluefaces yet?" the young woman asked him.

"Neither scale nor scutcheon of them. What manner of creature be they?"

She blinked her dark eyes. "They ain't got *no* manners to speak of."

"What I meant—"

"I know what you mean. They're scary, ugly blue guys with big feet and lots of teeth."

The young man who called himself Barnaby said, "That's about the size of it. No one knows what portal they came from. They began their attack about . . ." He scratched his head. "Jeez, Deena, how long has it been?"

She shook her head. "I dunno. It seems like days, but I know it hasn't been that long. Say ten hours."

"Has to be longer than that."

"Okay, say maybe twelve. Fifteen?"

"So, it's really just begun," Kwip ventured.

"Yeah, but how come you missed it?" Deena wanted to know.

"I was off in a far part of the castle. Outside the keep, along the outer walls. I had a fancy to explore some tall towers which stand thereabouts."

"Wow. You went wandering around alone? How'd you find your way there?"

"One gets used to the place. A servant showed me a tunnel betwixt the keep and the outer fortifications. I saw nothing of any disturbance."

Barnaby said, "Well, at least that means they haven't overrun the whole castle yet."

"'Twould be wondrous an they could. The castle's a vasty barn. Sometimes I think there's no end to it."

"I know what you mean. Still, the Bluefaces seem to be everywhere in the keep. At least that's the way it's appeared to us."

Kwip stroked his beard pensively. "Very likely you saw what you saw. They seem of a military bent, say you?"

"Very well organized, tactically pretty good, although they're not the best swordsmen in the world. It's just that they're very efficient soldiers."

"Such are dangerous, there's no doubt. Well, there seems to be nothing for it but to hie ourselves through a suitable aspect."

Barnaby nodded. "We tried to, but as you saw, our luck wasn't very good."

"No," Kwip agreed, "but I suspect inexperience were more the culprit than luck. There are any number of aspects. 'Tis but a matter of knowing which to choose."

"Well, we'd appreciate any help."

"Aye." Kwip was not keen on taking two fledglings under his wing. Such obligations tend to slow a man down. Still, he could not very well leave them to fend for themselves. He had no wish to trip across their corpses in a day or two. "I know a place," he said. "I sometimes take my mid-day meal there. It's well away from the Guests' quarters."

"Fine," Barnaby said. "We'd love to go along with you, if you'll have us."

"'Twould be my pleasure, sir."

See that you don't get underfoot, Kwip thought sourly. Damn me for a softhearted fool.

They exited the room and made their way down a narrow corridor which led to a short staircase. The stairs descended into a great hall furnished in chairs and tables and hung with colorful pennants. They moved through the room to a far door, which opened onto a hallway. Turning right, they walked a stretch, then swung left at an intersection.

"You seem to know where you're going," Barnaby observed.

"Be quiet!" Kwip whispered.

"Sorry," Barnaby mumbled.

Kwip held out an arm and Deena bumped into it, Barnaby bumping into her. Kwip tilted his head, listening a moment to far-off noises. Then he crooked two fingers and beckoned his companions forward again. They advanced down the hallway slowly.

A tremulous wail sounded in the distance. It was like nothing Kwip had ever heard. A chill went through him.

They stopped, Deena and Barnaby instinctively linking hands. Kwip turned to them.

"The invaders?" he asked quietly.

"I don't know," Barnaby said in an awed tone. "I can't imagine what *that* was. Sounded like some horrible . . . *thing*."

Kwip lifted his eyebrows, nodding emphatically. "Aye, it gave me a start. But many a strange beast walks this place." He drew his saber and motioned with his head. "Come on, then. And keep a sharp eye out."

They moved off. A few paces down they encountered a spiral stairwell. Kwip led them into it.

"I know a shortcut," he said.

They hurried down the well, their footsteps making hollow, muddled echoes against the curving stone walls.

They came out into one end of a long hallway, the T of a crossing passage a few paces to the left. Barnaby edged to the right, peering into a dark alcove across the way. Kwip decided to check out the intersection and peeked around the left corner.

Kwip had never seen a demon, but he knew the creature for what it was the moment he saw it. He could barely comprehend what he saw. It was big, about seven feet tall, and its head and face were a horror that he would half remember for nightmares without end. The eyes were not human, but seemed to radiate an intelligent malevolence like heat from the glowing tip of a torturer's pincer. The face was generally triangular, and the mouth gaped, heavy with numerous black, ragged teeth—charred stumps in a burnt forest. Its coloring was generally red, mottled with blotches of bilious green and diseased black. The torso and legs were powerfully muscled, and the three-toed feet ended in great curving talons. The area between its legs gave no hint of its gender, if it had one.

What Kwip found eye-defying was that the creature glowed with a strange interior light. The thing did not seem to be composed of ordinary matter. It was as if the figure were a three-dimensional painting, an artist's embodied rendering of a nightmare. A diffuse greenish glow surrounded the thing, and banners of shifting auroral color played about it here and there.

The sight hit Kwip as one telling blow. His pulse stopped, his blood froze, and his mind emptied of everything but a numbing fear.

The thing apparently had heard them coming out of the stairwell and had tried to creep up along the wall. It stopped when it saw Kwip, its mouth widening into a horrible travesty of a smile. Then it spoke one word.

"Death," it intoned. Part of the vibrations of which the voice was composed rumbled at the bottom end of the range of human hearing. The remaining, more audible component sounded like clustered notes pounded out on the lower octaves of a spinet's keyboard, combined with shrieking overtones that rasped against the ear.

Shocked into immobility, Kwip watched the thing raise a huge bladed weapon that was a cross between an ax and a scimitar. Faint multicolored flames played about the curious, evil-looking blade. The creature's glowing eyes nailed him with a look that pierced his heart, their hot, withering gaze searing the very nub of his being.

Hands yanked him back, and the demon's blade struck the wall at a point directly across from where his head had been. With a cascade of violet sparks, the stone fractured, pieces of it sailing off. Smoke rose from the impact point.

The next thing Kwip knew he was running faster than he had ever run in his life, and the thing was chasing him. He was dimly aware of the young man and woman running beside him.

They ran for a short eternity, the corridor an endless treadmill. Finally they reached the branches of a cross-tunnel.

"Split up!" Kwip shouted over his shoulder.

"Barnaby, this way!" Deena yelled, grabbing her fat friend's shirt sleeve and swinging him round. The two raced off down the left branch of the crossing.

The demon let them go and chased after Kwip.

LIBRARY

OSMIRIK WAS TIRED. He had lost track of time. It seemed that he had been locked in the vault for days on end. He had not slept yet, and his eyelids felt like lead weights. He forced himself to read on. There was no choice. Indeed, the fate of the castle might hang on what information he gleaned from the stacks of curious volumes that lay about the table.

So far, he had had no luck. Ervoldt's journal had proved a difficult read. The difficulty lay not so much in what the ancient King wrote as in what he omitted as irrelevant or of limited interest to the reader. What was sound editorial judgment on Ervoldt's part was vexatious obscurantism to the scholar. True, judicious paring had made for a lean and powerful narrative. Osmirik had marveled at the King's account of how he trapped the demon Ramthonodox and transmogrified it into a great castle. But exactly what supernatural means had he used to accomplish this feat? Ervoldt had written simply: "The Enchantment hath such Convolutions as to make the Brain fairly reel. I shall not bemuse the Reader by setting it down herewith."

Such bemusement was devoutly to be wished! But this was not the spell that Osmirik sought. There was another mentioned in the sections in which Ervoldt described his magical construct, Castle Perilous. The first of these chapters began with a typical understatement: "I found the Castle possessed of numerous Peculiarities."

Indeed. Ervoldt went on to describe the inherent dangers of the castle's unusual fenestration; Perilous had, in effect, 144,000 open windows, through which any manner of invader might trespass. There followed a catalogue of the aspects which the King explored, listing what was found therein and assessing its potential as a threat. The catalogue was short; apparently Ervoldt meant only to include a sample of what he had found. "It took me a Year and three-quarters, trudging through and through the Place. Much did I see." Obviously the King had covered a good deal of ground.

Ervoldt went on to describe some particularly troublesome aspects, outlining what measures he took to ensure that they would be no danger to the castle. There was one aspect which he had found especially alarming:

> I did then discover a Cosmos like no other I had seen. Vast and drear and fearful it was, a place of blackness and despair; yet Beings dwelled there, having such horrific Lineaments and foul Mien that I bethought them Demons, to be numbered among the very Hosts of Hell. I did but escape with my Life out of that Place, and laid a Spell of Entombment on the Way that led therein, and the Gods forfend its unbinding, at peril of the world—nay, of Creation itself! I say, beware this Place, in which is contained a surfeit of malign Cunning.

This was the only reference Ervoldt made to the Hosts of Hell, and to the nature of the spells used to seal off especially dangerous aspects. Osmirik had searched through volume after volume of arcane magic, chasing down spells similarly named. He had found restraining spells, binding spells, immobility spells, and confinement spells, but nothing that carried the connotation of the Haplan verb *tymbut*, which Osmirik had translated as meaning "to place within a tomb or burial place." Ervoldt's offhand mention suggested that the spell was common, one that could be found in the standard spell manuals of the day. Indeed, the King had mentioned other sorts of spells, and those Osmirik had located. But he could find no trace of a spell specifically designed for the purpose of sealing something or someone in a tomb or burial place.

It was a puzzle. Why would Ervoldt use a spell of this kind?

What, indeed, could be the common use of such a curious enchantment? Why would anyone be interested in sealing the dead inside their tombs? It was a common practice to equip burial places with magical defenses to ward off ghouls and grave robbers, but these certainly were not meant to inhibit the dead from getting up and walking out. . . .

Osmirik rubbed his eyes and looked about the tiny, candlelit chamber. He had stacked almost two hundred books inside it, and he had just about riffled through them all. He sighed, leaned back, and stretched his arms, his cramped muscles throbbing. Then he gave a protracted yawn. It would be so good to lay his head down on the table, just for a moment, just to rest. . . .

No. Lord Incarnadine had charged him with this vital mission, and he could not fail his sovereign liege.

He groped in the satchel for something to eat, coming up with a loaf of bread and a wedge of cheese. He used his dagger to slice the cheese, hands to tear off a chunk of bread. There was a bottle of wine under the table, but he was wary of opening it. A few good swallows, and he'd be out like a candle.

He ate voraciously at first, then slowed down as his mind returned to the problem at hand. Had live entombment been a common capital punishment in ancient times? If so, it was not widely known, but would explain Ervoldt's not bothering to be specific about the method used. Of course, he may have wanted to keep the spell a secret to guard against someone's tampering with it.

Of course. That had to be the reason. Still, it could be a simple and fairly common enchantment. . . .

Something clicked inside his mind. The only motivation for laying such a spell on a tomb would be an inordinate fear of the dead. Necrophobia was widespread in ancient times, and was no rarity even today. The ancient Hunrans, who were in Ervoldt's day called Tryphosites, had a cult of the dead—rather the opposite of a cult, for the Tryphosites believed that those who died became evil spirits in the afterlife, occasionally returning to Earth to work their devilment on the living.

Yes!

He tossed the bread and cheese aside. If Ervoldt had used an existing spell, he might have borrowed it from the Tryphosites, whose magic he must have studied.

Osmirik slammed his bony fist against the table. There was a book on Tryphosite magic in the library. But he would have to leave the vault to fetch it! That would be the bravest of deeds. The blue-skinned Hosts of Hell were certainly out there. Yet he had to do it. He had to run the risk of losing his immortal spirit to demons from the fiery bowels of Perdition.

Something nagged at him—a triviality, really. The blue creatures had not struck him as proper-looking demons. They were brutish, monstrous, and ugly as sin—but not quite what one would expect of genuine evil spirits.

No matter. They were dreadful enough. So be it.

He rose and went to the outside wall, feeling along the stone ribbing for the switch that would send the stone slab rolling back into its slot in the wall. He found it and rested two tremulous fingers on it.

A cold sweat broke out along his forehead. Keeping his fingers lightly on the switch, he bent and blew out the candle.

It was worse in the dark. He did not know if he could bring himself to do it. Could he face Evil itself? Could any mortal? He stood awhile in agonized indecision. Then he lowered his hand.

He groped along the table for the flint wheel, found it, and struck a spark. The oil-soaked cotton flamed, and he lit the candle.

He would have his last meal, then venture out of the vault to meet his fate. Surely no one could expect him to face an eternity of torment on an empty stomach. Besides, he needed time to cogitate. There must be an alternative, one he was simply not thinking of.

Now where the devil was that bottle of wine . . .?

PENNSYLVANIA

THE TEMPERATURE ROSE a bit as they drove farther west and crossed a weather front, but it was still chilly. The sky was cloudless, spangled with cold winter stars. The road wound through dale and over hill, farmlets sleeping to either side. An occasional dimly lighted window alleviated the darkness, the loneliness.

"Do you know exactly where Ferne's estate is?"

"I'll be able to pinpoint the gateway," Trent said, "which amounts to the same thing."

Incarnadine looked out into the darkness. "Bleak," he said.

"What do you expect for the wilds of Pennsylvania on a winter night?"

"A roaring fire, a bottle of good wine, some good music. . . ."

"Sounds nice. Want to bag out of this and go and get some of that good stuff?"

"I could hardly do that."

Trent shrugged. "Let the gods-damned castle go to the devil. Choose a world and live in it, never leave."

"I've often considered it."

"Do it. Let Ferne have the old rat trap, let her be Queen of Creation."

Incarnadine took a long breath. "What you said about going to the devil—it's looking more and more as though that might be literally true."

"Well, that demon semi back there wasn't Ferne's style, if that's what you mean." Trent flicked on the high beams, and the trees along the road loomed like tall gray specters. "Do you really think it's the Hosts of Hell?"

"I have no doubt. Naturally they'll be laying for me—us—at the portal. We'll need all the magic you can muster. Otherwise, we're sunk."

"Well, I hope I'll be able to summon the portal when we get close to it. Going to be rough, though. They've got it nailed down pretty tight on this end."

"Do you think proximity will make any difference?"

"Hard to say. All I know is that doing it from New York was impossible."

They came into a small town, turning left at a junction with another highway. Now and then, pairs of headlights came at them, receded into the night.

"Getting close?" Incarnadine asked.

"Yeah. It's off on your side somewhere."

A turnoff to the right came up and Trent took it. The road took a slight dip directly off the highway, then bore gradually uphill, a split-rail fence running along its right side. They passed a very large and very imposing stone barn, then a few other outbuildings.

"Some big farms around here."

"Gentlemen farmers, it looks like," Trent said. "The country estates of the super-rich."

Other farms rolled by. Trent took a side road to the left that arched over a hill, then ran along a winding valley, crossing a stream via a stone bridge. Then it twined upward through stark, bare-limbed trees. They went by the entrance to a gravel-paved side road that was barred by a steel-pipe gate. A mailbox stood off to one side.

A quarter mile farther down the road, Trent said, "That was it."

"Are you sure?"

"Yes. Want to try a head-on assault?"

"No. That gate looked pretty sturdy. Let's see if we can't find a hole in their perimeter defenses."

The road branched and they bore to the right. The road wound through forest, a chain link fence paralleling it on the right.

"This looks like the back end of the property," Incarnadine said.

"That fence doesn't seem like much," Trent observed. "Not even barbed wire along the top. Electrified, maybe."

"I doubt it."

"Then they must be confident of their magical defenses."

"One would tend to think so, if that big ghostly rig was any indication."

Trent pulled off the road, parked on the narrow cinder-strewn shoulder, and turned off the motor. He doused the headlights. Quiet fell, save for the sound of a cold wind through the treetops.

"Want to try it right here?"

"Well, not in the car."

They left the Mercedes and walked to the chain link fence. Trent raised his arms and traced small circles with his index fingers, looking off, as if testing.

"This is going to be difficult." He looked around. "Hate to do it in the open like this. If somebody comes along . . ."

"They'll be mighty suspicious but will probably drive on. Let's give it a try."

Trent nodded, then began to trace elaborate patterns in the air. After a time, thin suspended filaments of light appeared, taking their shape from the path of his fingers, forming a luminous grid that hung between the two brothers.

"Nope." He lowered his arms and examined the pattern. He was not satisfied. "No. It won't work. They have it anchored too firmly. They own the door, Inky. And they have the key. We'll simply have to go in there and crash it down."

"So be it. Are you ready?"

With one finger, Trent drew a diagonal slash across the pattern: the Stroke of Cancellation. The luminous design faded quickly. "As ready as one can be to die, which is what the upshot of this enterprise is likely to be. But first, let me deal with this fence business."

Trent waved out a simple pattern, and the fence took it upon itself to give up a few of its chain links, to the accompaniment of much clinking and snapping of metal. A section of steel mesh split down the middle and fell away like a torn curtain.

"Neat," Incarnadine admired.

They walked through the gap and into the woods, following a

winding deer trail. About fifty yards along they encountered a clearing. In the lead, Trent stopped.

"One other thing I can do is give us some power. We're going to need a shitload of it. I'm going to tune it so that you can channel it for any weapon or defense you see fit to use. So just wish, and it shall be done. Think you can handle that?"

Incarnadine smiled crookedly. "Two days ago I couldn't even spell 'magician.' Now I are one."

Trent stepped back and again began to make motions with his hands. At length the pattern became visible. It was wondrously complex, comprising red, blue, and green filaments. Arcane geometric figures decorated with elaborate filigree took shape within it, along with subtle curves describing arcs of mathematical precision and elegance.

A high-pitched, agonized yowl, as from a strange, half-human creature, came from somewhere ahead. Various grunting and snorting sounds arose from the woods.

"The natives are having nervous breakdowns," Incarnadine muttered.

After a time, the filaments all turned bright blue, growing brighter as the seconds passed. Trent worked furiously, eyes caged on his work, his pale brow furrowed, fingers flying. Incarnadine took a step back as the pattern began to emit great waves of heat. The filaments turned blue-white and kept increasing in luminosity. Finally they became stark, blinding white, humming and crackling with energy.

Finished at last, Trent staggered back, flinching from the intense heat. "Gods!" He wiped the film of sweat from his forehead.

"I'm impressed," Incarnadine said, studying the pattern. "That's the hairiest-looking Power Grid I've ever seen. Three-dimensional, too! How the hell did you execute all those icosahedrons so quickly?"

"I nearly burned my damn face off doing it." Trent exhaled slowly, straightening his clothes. "But she'll hold for hours." He glanced around. "It's rained recently, so there isn't much chance of a fire unless we overload it."

The roar of some great, hellish beast rent the night.

"That is a distinct possibility," Incarnadine said, looking off into the darkness.

"The only thing that will save us," Trent said, "*might* save us, is that they will be dealing with the same unfavorable conditions, with respect to magic in general, as we. On the down side, they seemed to have learned very quickly.''

. They left the anomaly blazing behind them like an overloaded Art Deco neon sign. The deer trail continued for another twenty yards, debouching into a hayfield that slanted up a low rise. They struck out into the open, crushing dry, brittle grass underfoot. Light came from over the rise, outlining the top of the hill.

''We should stick to cover,'' Trent said.

''I suspect they know exactly where we are. Whoever or whatever we have to face, we might as well face them in the open.''

Weighty footsteps sounded just over the hill, along with a deep-throated growl. Then a ferocious saurian head appeared above the line of the hilltop, its fiery eyes sweeping the field below. The rest of the monster came into view as it topped the rise. At least twenty feet tall, it vaguely resembled a Tyrannosaurus rex, but differed chiefly by virtue of its fully prehensile, thickly muscled upper limbs, at the ends of which sprouted huge curving talons. Its eyes glowed like yellow beacons, and faint red flames shot from its mouth as it took each whistling breath.

''On second thought,'' Incarnadine said.

They dashed off in opposite directions, both heading for woods on either side. The monster swung its gaze between them, pondering which quarry would make the tastiest morsel.

Then it made its decision and sprang forward to give chase.

CASTLE

THEY FOUND MORE dead Bluefaces everywhere they went. Blue corpses littered the rooms and corridors, lay like butchered meat in the great halls and stairwells. They marveled at the slaughter, surprised to be feeling a tinge of pity. It seemed certain that none of the invaders were left alive. If any had survived, they were likely in hiding or had beat a hasty retreat back to their world.

"Serves 'em right, I guess," Gene said.

"They didn't have to kill all of them," Linda said.

"Yeah, but who are 'they'?"

"Good fighters," Snowclaw commented.

Gene whistled. "Sure are. That means we're in a worse situation than we were with these guys."

"Same difference," Linda said. "Both ways, we're out of the castle."

"I don't know," Gene said as he bent to inspect a charred and blackened corpse. "Incarnadine and his Guard might have been able to take the castle back from the Bluefaces. But against whoever or whatever did this, I'm a little pessimistic of their chances. Very pessimistic, actually."

They walked on a little farther, coming into a large empty dining hall. A few more dismembered cadavers lay about.

"We'd better find a good aspect fast," Gene said, keeping his voice low. "I think this is the King's Hall. Isn't it?"

"Looks like. That means we're near the Guest areas," Linda said. "But I don't see a darn thing."

"Let's get the hell away from here and back into the wild regions."

"But we need a stable aspect."

"I think it's boiling down to this—we're going to have to pick the least objectionable wild aspect we can find and make the best of it. I really think the castle is a lost cause."

Linda's face fell. "I suppose you're right."

"But before we do that, we have to make sure that this carnage *isn't* the work of the King and his Guardsmen."

"Do you think there's a chance?" Sheila asked.

"No. But we have to be absolutely positive before we exile ourselves again."

"We might be better off back in the jungle," Linda said. "If it weren't for Snowy not being able to take the heat."

"Linda's right," Snowclaw said. "Don't put yourselves in danger on my account. Go back to that place. With Sheila along, you'll be able to get back into the castle anytime you like. I'll stay here and scout around."

"I can't take the heat, either," Gene said. "Sorry, Snowclaw, that's real noble of you, but I'm not going to leave you here alone."

"Remember," Snowclaw said, "I have a stable aspect to slip into anytime I want."

Gene laughed. "I thought you said you couldn't make it back in the real world?"

"Well, maybe I did, and maybe I can't. But it's no big thing one way or the other. Actually I never really—"

Snowy was silenced by a horrible, blood-chilling yell that seemed to echo throughout the castle. They all stopped, stunned by the sound of it.

It took a few moments before any of them could speak. "My God," Linda whispered, her face gone a bit gray. "Gene, what was it?"

"Uh . . . I hope I never find out. This way."

Gene led them down a short hallway that made an L to the left. After peeking around the corner, he beckoned to his companions, and they followed him up another short corridor, passing a stairwell.

The horrible yowl came again, and this time it seemed to boom from around the corner ahead. They hastily backtracked and took the stairwell, which led up. But more strange cries assailed their ears up on the next floor, so they climbed six more flights until the sounds diminished.

Linda gasped, "Think . . . think we're safe?"

"I dunno," Gene said, a little out of breath.

More bellowing came to their ears, but from a distance.

"Maybe," Gene said. "Whatever that is, I do not want to meet up with it."

"You mean with them," Sheila said. "It sounds like there are hundreds of them, all over."

"I don't want to think about that today," Gene said airily. "After all, tomorrow is another day. I think." He slapped himself on the face. "Shut up, you're babbling."

"I'm going nuts, too," Linda said. "Gene, I'm scared. I want to get out of here."

"Righto! We'll take the first portal." He looked around and gave a sardonic grunt. "Wouldn't you know, when you *need* one of the goddamn things, suddenly everything's normal. Like Sunday in the park."

Sheila began, "I think . . ." Then she trailed off.

They waited. Then Gene said, "What is it, Sheila?"

Sheila closed her eyes, holding her breath. She held it for a good fifteen seconds. Then she breathed out and opened her eyes, looking disappointed. "Thought I had it. For a second there, anyway."

"Keep working on it. I'm for heading that way, folks, but if anyone has a better idea, I believe in democracy and the principle of one man, one vote. Or one being, one vote."

Everyone accepted Gene's autocracy and followed him down the dim corridor. They crept along, wary of every shadow, Sheila hanging on to a tuft of Snowy's fur.

Gene saw something ahead and stopped, holding out a hand. A strange, hulking shadow lay across the floor, the thing it shadowed obviously standing just around the corner. The thing, whatever it was, stood motionless.

They flattened against the wall and froze. Sheila could hear her heart banging against her sternum like some wild frightened thing. She felt only numbness and an overwhelming sense that they would never get out of the castle alive. This was it; this was the end of her life. And she could not bring herself to be frightened.

Silence hung like a boulder precariously balanced. Then a rumbling murmur came from around the corner. It rose in pitch to become something far removed from a human voice yet somehow akin to it, eventually turning into an evil chuckling, a mocking laugh.

Then the form stepped out from behind the corner. The eyes of it were evil, and held them all. It raised its fiery sword.

Linda screamed. Gene's hand went to his sword but he had trouble pulling it free, as if his arm had suddenly turned to rubber.

Snowy charged past and engaged the thing. Metal clashed and sparks flew. Snowy exchanged a few strokes with it before the blade of his longsword snapped in two, singing its distress as it glanced off the wall and clattered to the floor. The demon swung viciously and Snowy jumped, doing two quick backward somersaults before rolling to his feet. A long diagonal line of singed fur ran across his chest, wisps of smoke rising from it.

"Run, everybody!" Snowy yelled.

They needed no coaxing. Sheila ran as fast as she had ever run in her life, even passing up Snowclaw. A demonic howl came at their backs and sped them on.

It took some time to realize that the demon had stopped chasing them, possibly because the answering cry of one of his comrades came from up ahead. Two huge wooden doors lay at the end of an alcove to the left, and they all ducked through into a huge room full of books. One of the doors had a hole in it, looking to have been battered in. Gene and Snowy slammed the doors shut, then began piling heavy wooden tables in front of them, laying the first on its side to block the hole in the door.

Soon the pile of tables and chairs mounted beyond the top of the doors. Snowy was about to throw the last of the oak tables on top of the pile when there was a flash and the pile flew to splinters amid a shower of sparks. The smoke cleared, revealing two demons with fiery swords standing just outside the doorway. They bellowed triumphantly and jumped forward.

A huge steel door materialized in front of them, sealing off the entrance.

"That ought to hold the bastards!" Linda screamed, then burst into tears.

Gene held her, watching the door, listening to the loud banging sounds that had begun, coming from the other side.

"They'll cut through that steel eventually," he said.

"It's two feet thick," Linda said, drying her eyes. "Oh, Gene, they're the evilest things in the world. Horrible, horrible—"

"They won't get us, Linda. I promise. I won't let them."

They all backed away from the door. Sheila clung to Snowclaw, wanting to lose herself in the forest of his warm fur. She noticed the smell of burnt hair and ran her hand across the burn along his chest.

"Snowy, you're hurt."

"Nah, just got singed a little."

More horrendous banging sounded, but the door seemed to be holding for the moment.

It hit Sheila suddenly. She couldn't put it into words if she tried for a year, but something had happened. She understood the magic of the castle. It was like noticing a huge feature of the landscape for the first time, something so big and obvious that you wondered why you hadn't noticed it before.

She let go of Snowclaw. "Gene! I have it figured out! I can summon the portal!"

Gene nodded understandingly. "Do so. Like, immediately."

"Uh . . . oh. Yeah, sure!"

Sheila looked around. The library was huge. The main floor held rows and rows of open shelves stacked with books. There were more shelves spaced around the walls, interspersed with study nooks and carrels. Above were two stories of galleries, with more shelving and still more books. Other, smaller side rooms let off the main floor, and she crossed to one of these, stopping in front of the high pointed arch that formed its entrance. The arch would make a good frame for the edges of the portal.

Now all she had to do was summon the portal. Easy in principle, but now that she thought about it, her general knowledge of the castle's magic would have to be refined and adapted for this particular job. It would take some time.

A fearful crash sounded, and the steel doors shook.

Sheila turned back to her task. She would have to learn her new magic *real fast*.

ESTATE

.

As INCARNADINE, LORD of the Western Pale, sprinted for the woods, he wondered which way of dying would be the quickest and least painful: being crushed to death under huge reptilian feet, being burned to char, or being eaten alive, torn apart in the maw of the gargantuan creature that was now chasing him. The question was academic, inasmuch as the creature would most likely combine all three methods. First tenderize the meat, parbroil it to taste, then gobble it down after a few brisk chews.

Flames from the creature licked at his back. Something crackled around his head, and he realized his hair was on fire. Slapping at his head, he willed a forfending shield to cover him and hoped it would be efficacious.

He dove into the woods and hid behind a stout oak, peering around its trunk. The monster was temporarily blocked by the trees. It roared out its disappointment over losing a quick meal, streams of thin red flame shooting from its nostrils. Then, extending its upper limbs, it took hold of two birch trees and pried them apart. The trees snapped like matchsticks and fell over. The monster began to bull its way into the woods, branches snapping as it moved.

Incarnadine examined the hand-held missile launcher that had materialized in his grasp. It was a long tube affair, set about with gadgets and gizmos. It was very heavy. He studied it for a moment. He was not familiar with its type, but the device did not look overcomplicated. Probably a Soviet design. He balanced the tube on his shoulder and put his eye to the aiming scope. He centered the beast's thorax in the cross hairs and waited for a clear shot. Finally getting one, he squeezed the trigger-grip.

The missile whooshed away, spewing yellow flame and leaving noxious fumes in its wake. Incarnadine did not see it hit, but heard the explosion.

When the smoke cleared, he saw that the beast was down, its massive head wedged between two tree trunks, the glow of its yellow eyes dimming quickly. Then, suddenly, the huge animal vanished with a bright flash. Nothing remained but trailing smoke.

The missile launcher also disappeared, but with less fanfare. Incarnadine walked out of the woods and rejoined his brother on the meadow.

"Nice solution," Trent said.

"Thanks. Better than conjuring a knight atop a foaming charger, or some such poetry."

"Whatever it takes."

They advanced up the sloping meadow, soon reaching the crest of the hill. Below them stood a large manor house done in the Tudor style, surrounded by trees, gardens, and numerous outbuildings. Dim light glowed behind curtained windows in the main house.

"So far, so good," Trent said. "What next, I wonder?"

As if in answer, a bright green shaft of energy lanced out from what looked like a large toolshed near the house. A blinding green aura enveloped the two brothers, outlining the bell-shaped forfending shields around each of them.

Trent made circles with his index fingers, moving first clockwise, then counter. "Okay, they don't have enough power here to get through our shields using the fancy high-tech stuff."

"Maybe we have a ghost of a chance after all."

"Maybe. The stuff they do have is nothing to sneeze at. Looks like it might boil down to swordplay, though. I can't figure it. They must not be connected to their continuum."

"Hope springs eternal. I thought they'd be running a channel right through the castle to here."

"That's what I figured. But maybe Ferne's still holding out."

"I don't see how she could be," Incarnadine said. "But more power to her. For the moment."

Another bolt, this one a bright magenta, shot out from the trees.

"Testing different frequencies," Trent said. "Maybe they'll find one that works. In the meantime, this will keep them honest."

Trent raised his arm and pointed at the source of the firing. A blue-white shaft of energy speared out from his fingertip and hit the shed, which disintegrated in a fiery explosion.

"Good shooting," Incarnadine said.

A sudden droning came from above—the motor of a plane. Looking up, they could see its outline against the stars. The plane banked, then went into a screaming dive.

"Sounds like a Stuka," Trent said. "The bombs we can live with, but it could strafe us with silver bullets."

Tiny sparks of flame budded along the black outline of the bomber, and the rattle of machine guns sounded. A few slugs chunked into the earth at Incarnadine's feet.

Behind them, something rose from the trees on a pillar of fire and streaked into the night, heading along a collision course with the plane. Within a few seconds, missile and plane met in the air about midway between the house and the top of the knoll. A brilliant starburst of light blossomed at their joining. Almost simultaneously, a huge explosion tore up the meadow about twenty yards in front of where the brothers stood. A second bomb hit just behind them, splattering chunks of frozen brown earth.

"Think we should take cover?" Incarnadine asked when the smoke and dust had cleared.

"Not yet. I can't say I've been really impressed by anything so far."

"You didn't have that reptile chasing you."

"I concede the point. But I wonder why they're holding back? Toying with us?"

"Trent, it may just be that they're as chary of us as we are of them."

"Gee, think of that. Let's get closer."

"Hold on."

Many things began to happen. Great winged beasts appeared, defecating balls of fire as they flapped their huge pinions overhead. A motley troop of creatures—variously taloned and beaked, chitinous and scutellate, some with claws, others with pinchers—began charging up the hill. Amorphous shapes slithered out of shadow, leaping and gibbering. Vapors coalesced and churned with demonic energy, advancing like tornadoes. The grass was alive with fang-bearing homunculi that screamed and chittered their venomous hatred.

"A shooting gallery!" Trent said, both index fingers raised and spewing multicolored fire. "Have fun!"

"It may be our last chance," Incarnadine said as his first shot dehorned a seven-foot-tall ambulatory crustacean with delusions of horror-film stardom.

The spooks charged and the bolts flew. Smoke and fire rose from the hayfield as chitin smoldered and scales burned. Great flying creatures plummeted from the sky, trailing pink and yellow sparks and bright blue smoke. Vortexes exploded, and brilliant shafts of radiant energy intersected in the night. There came swarming congeries of fiery motes, and bright tongues of flame, the sky taking its color from their flashing luminescence.

Incarnadine flamed a four-pincered lobsterlike thing that had advanced to within a few yards of him, and when the creature vanished in a puff of vermilion smoke, the armored, insectoid little hellion that it had shielded leaped at him like a grasshopper. He fired, diving to the right and rolling to his feet again, only to confront another hobgoblin, this one a nine-foot-tall cross between a praying mantis and a sexually aroused ostrich. Incarnadine hosed it down, then played his beam of energy on the blasphemous horror that wriggled and twitched behind it.

The battle continued for some time, stratagems being employed on both sides. Creatures would feint at one invader and charge the other. The brothers cross-fired on oversize and airborne demons, and generally helped each other when they could.

Eventually the stream of apparitions petered out.

Incarnadine burned the last of the big ones, then mopped up what remained of the salamanders and other smaller incubi.

When done, he turned to see Trent shaking off a small legless thing with big yellow teeth that was worrying at the cuff of his trousers. He kicked it away and spritzed it with fire. The thing squealed hideously, blazing into nothingness like a scrap of flash paper.

Trent walked over to his brother, smiling, his breath trailing behind him in the cold night air. "So much for the fireworks. I wonder when the real battle's going to start?"

Something was forming in the air over the manor house, something big. It was an image, at first blurred and indistinct, gradually growing sharper.

It was a face, a human face, dark of eye and square of jaw. The thin lips curled into a pleasant smile.

"Hi!" the image said brightly. "Listen. Can we talk?"

CASTLE

"HOW'S IT LOOK out there?" Barnaby whispered.

Deena poked her head out of the niche and looked up and down the corridor.

"Okay. I don't see any of 'em."

"Let's move."

Cautiously they exited the niche and inched along the wall, their eyes wide and fearful. A demon howled somewhere close, and they froze.

Deena pushed her face against Barnaby's chest. "They gonna get us," she whimpered.

"No!" Barnaby said. "We're going to get out of here. Let's move."

Deena dried her eyes and crept on.

Barnaby stayed behind for a moment, looking back down the passageway. Deena reached back for his hand, couldn't find it, and halted, turning her head.

"Barnaby!"

"Shh. Hold it."

"C'mon!"

Satisfied that they weren't being followed, he started forward. Deena took a step, bringing her head around in time to see a human hand growing out of the wall.

She screamed and jumped back.

The hand grew an arm, which in turn got connected to a shoulder. Then Kwip stepped out of the wall like a ghost in the flesh.

The two were dumbfounded.

Kwip put a finger to his lips. "It's me peculiar talent. I'm glad to find you."

"How did you get away from that . . . thing?" Barnaby asked.

"The demon? By the method you just saw. I've the Creator to thank that wall-walking's a talent they lack."

"Can we still get to that aspect of yours? Do you know where we are?"

"Approximately. Methinks we'd best hide out awhile. A blind chamber, preferably with something to eat and drink in it, a wine and cheese cellar, perhaps. But any room with a locked door will do."

"Sounds good to me," Deena said.

"Aye. Now, do exactly as I say. Come here, lad." He drew Barnaby to him by the hand. "Take hold of the back of me shirt and hang on for dear life. Join hands with your ladyfriend, and whatever you do, don't let go of her, either. Am I clear?"

They nodded.

"Good. Now, follow me, and hesitate at peril of your life."

They lined up, Kwip in front facing the wall.

A hellish screeching came from the left. They turned to see a demon rushing down the passageway at them.

"Follow me!" Kwip shouted, striding forward. He merged with the stone and was absorbed into it. Unbelieving but unwilling to be left behind, Barnaby and Deena followed.

The passage through the stone was like walking in water. Mercifully the experience was of short duration. They emerged into another hallway.

"That was *weird*," Deena said.

Kwip glanced around. "And again."

They ghosted through the opposite wall. This time they came out in a book-crammed chamber lit by a single candle that had almost burned itself out.

Kwip barked a shin against the tome-littered table that filled most of the floor space. "Gods of a pig's arse!" Rubbing his leg, he looked around. "Well, food for thought, at any rate. This will do, I suppose. No demon will get in here."

They heard a disgruntled moan. It had come from beneath the table.

Kwip drew his saber, knocking over a stack of books. Then a head appeared above the tabletop. The glazed eyes of a slight, balding man regarded the intruders.

"Greetings." The man belched. "If you don't mind my asking, how in the name of all the gods did you get in here?"

"It's the librarian," Kwip told his companions.

Osmirik squinted at him. "Kwip. Ah, Kwip, my good man." Osmirik struggled to his feet. Tongue a trifle thick, he licked his lips, scratching himself. Smiling, he said, "I'm glad for a little company. It was getting a bit lonely in here."

"Hiding out, then?" Kwip asked, sheathing his sword.

"Quite so. Ah, I see I have more than one guest." Osmirik smiled.

Barnaby introduced himself and Deena.

"Enchanted, my dear lady," Osmirik said, overdoing a bow. He was obviously a bit drunk.

Deena giggled, but enjoyed the scribe's elaborate gesture.

He continued, "An honor, goodly sir. Welcome to my humble lodgings, such as they are. There is food aplenty, if you wish refreshment, but I'm afraid I have nothing to offer you to drink." He held up the empty wine bottle and regarded it with much puzzlement, as if there were some question as to how the contents had disappeared.

"Thanks. We'd love some food," Barnaby said. "Is it safe here? Have you seen the demons?"

The librarian's face blanched. "I've seen them, sure enough."

"Here?"

"Not here. Those foul blue hellions won't get through that wall. It's as thick as a—"

"Blue hellions?" Kwip said.

"The demons. Blue creatures with intensively redundant dentition. Didn't you—?"

"Those ain't the demons," Deena said. "You obviously ain't seen no demons yet. When you see one you'll know."

Osmirik sat down, looking grave. "I will?"

"Other beings have invaded the castle," Barnaby said. "These things are indescribably worse."

"Indescribably . . .?" Osmirik paled and reached for the wine bottle. Spying the dregs at the bottom, he upended the bottle into his mouth. He wiped his lips. "Demons or none, my duty is clear. I must venture out and get the volume."

Kwip looked at him incredulously. "Gods of a spavined nag. How the devil can you think of books at a time like this?"

"I must have the spell to give to my liege lord, Incarnadine."

"What spell?"

"The spell that will close up the demons' aspect. Seal it off, so they can't get through. I need the book that contains that spell."

Kwip nodded, rolling his eyes in appreciation. "Aye. Now, there's a book worth considerable thought. Whereabouts is it?"

"Out there," Osmirik said, pointing to the wall sealing off the arch.

"The library?"

"Aye, down in the open stacks. I must fetch it, be there demons or be there none."

"Well, there's but one way to decide aye or nay. I'll have a look-see."

"Be careful, they may see you!"

Kwip gave a wry smile. "I'm a man who doesn't fancy being seen. Never fear."

He drew up to the section of wall within the arch, stopping just short of touching it with his nose. He leaned forward, and his head and the top half of his torso disappeared into the wall.

He remained in this paradoxical state, half in and half out, for a longish moment. Then he pulled back.

"Something's up," he said, a strange expression on his face. "Abide. I shall return shortly."

He walked through the wall and was gone.

LIBRARY

SHEILA STOOD WITH her eyes closed and her arms straight down and rigid, fists clenched and knuckles white. She swayed from side to side like a sapling in a mild breeze. The others stood by and watched. Snowclaw reached out for her as she swayed, but stopped short of touching her.

They heard someone walking above, and turned to look. Gene drew his sword. The clanging and banging on the other side of the huge steel doors continued.

Smiling, Kwip came out of the stairwell to the first gallery. Linda and Gene met him halfway across the floor.

"Fancy you people being here," Kwip said. "How goes the world with you?"

"Not too darn good," Gene said. "Were you hiding out in here?"

"For the nonce, yes. I've been away. Apparently there's been trouble."

"A lot of it. Have you seen the demons?"

"Aye, and nearly soiled my breeches."

"Well, get out a fresh pair of undies, because they're right behind that door, making all the racket."

"Gods of a pig's arse! Then we'd best take our leave, hadn't we?"

"We're working on it. That girl there has a powerful talent. She can summon portals."

"The devil you say." Kwip looked over his shoulder.

"Well, she did it once. She's trying like hell to repeat it."

They watched Sheila teeter gently back and forth.

"I'd best go fetch them," Kwip said, then answered Gene's questioning look with, "The librarian and some others. I'll be back in a trice." He trotted back to the stairwell.

A loud bang sounded. Gene and Linda looked back at the steel barrier. A large protrusion had appeared on it, as if something had nearly punched through from the other side.

Another door materialized, covering the existing one.

"I can keep whipping up doors as long as we stay here," Linda said, "but once we cross the portal . . ."

"Yeah, and they'll follow us through." Gene bit his lip. "I hadn't considered that. Good God, can you imagine those things loose on Earth?"

"I don't want to think about it. Gene, we can't take the chance of summoning the portal!"

A wave of heat hit them. The clanging and banging had ceased, and now thin streamers of smoke rose from the door.

"Hell. They're burning their way through! Linda, we have to get out of here. Maybe Sheila can make the portal go away after we cross over."

"Let's hope so, or else we'll be responsible for the destruction of our world."

The door was glowing a deep cherry-red. Linda covered it with another layer of solid steel. The barrier now jutted out from the wall a good six feet. The heat dissipated momentarily, but then returned.

"That won't hold them very long," Linda said.

"Look!"

Linda whirled. The alcove that Sheila stood in front of seemed to have undergone a transformation. Then Linda realized that she was looking through a portal.

Kwip came out of the stairwell, followed by Barnaby Walsh, Deena Williams, and Osmirik the librarian. Without uttering a word of greeting or explanation, Osmirik broke for the open stacks.

"Hey!" Gene yelled, then turned to Kwip. "Where the hell is he going?"

"To fetch an important book."

"Book? Tell him we have to—"

"It's vital, trust me," Kwip said.

"Well, if you say so."

They all peered through the portal. On the other side was a pleasantly and expensively appointed living room. The walls were of dark wood paneling, the ceiling of dark oak beams. It looked like the interior of an English manor house.

"Looks like Earth," Gene said, smiling at Sheila. "Good work."

Sheila nodded. "It was pretty tough. Seemed like something was holding it back. Like someone had tied it down somewhere else in the castle."

"Maybe. I wonder where it's been hiding all this time?" He shook his head in wonder. "There it is. Home. God, I can't believe it."

Sheila glanced at the barrier, which had again turned red-hot. "I have to stay."

"Are you nuts?"

"No. I have to close up the portal from this side. I won't be able to do magic on the other side. It's outside the castle, remember?"

"But you found your magic outside the castle. Look, Sheila. I haven't given this a lot of thought yet, but obviously you're a major talent. Maybe your talent isn't limited to summoning portals. You also seem to have the knack for figuring out alternative magical systems, for want of a better way to put it."

Sheila thought about it. "Maybe I do."

"I think you could figure out Earth's system easy."

"If I have enough time, maybe," Sheila said. "But we can't take the chance. What if they get through?"

Gene grabbed her arm. "Look, there's no way I'm going to let you stay behind and face those things alone."

"No, Gene. It has to be. You take Linda back."

"Nothing doing. You're coming with us."

"Gene, I can't."

The ear-splitting groan of tortured metal filled the library. The door had turned white-hot.

"Sheila, go with him," Linda said. "I've rigged something up to buy us time."

They turned. The portal now looked like a bank deposit vault.

An enormous steel door with a complex locking mechanism hung open on gimbals.

"It's three feet thick," Linda said. "It's set to close in fifteen seconds. Sheila, you'll have about five minutes to learn Earth magic. Run, everybody!"

Snowclaw, Linda, Barnaby, and Deena ran. Kwip, Gene, and Sheila stayed.

Gene said, "Look, if the demons take over the castle, Earth's done for."

"I suppose you're right."

An explosion rocked the place. Shards of molten metal spewed from a small hole that had appeared in the barrier blocking the library entrance.

Gene and Sheila ran for the portal. Kwip waited for Osmirik, who came charging out of the open stacks, book in hand.

When they reached the other side, everyone watched the huge steel door swing shut. It closed with a slam, and the complex locking mechanism hummed and whirred for a moment. Then it fell silent.

A few seconds later, the vault door disappeared. Through the portal lay a room somewhere in the castle. It was furnished with antiques and decorated with tapestries and other curios. A strikingly attractive woman in a dark red gown stepped into the frame of the aspect. Startled, she halted, regarding the group of strangers on the other side with some astonishment.

"Who in Creation might you people be?" she asked.

"We might ask the same of you," Gene said.

She stiffened. "Such impertinence. What are you doing in my house? Where are my servants?"

"Look, lady, we just missed being devil's food cake by a short hair. The demons were right behind us."

Her eyebrows shot up. "Demons? Where did you see them?"

"We just came from the castle."

"So it was you who moved this end of the portal. How did you manage it?" She cut short any answer with a wave of her hand. "Never mind. You must leave my house immediately. I cannot let you re-enter the castle this way. We are under attack here."

"We know. We don't want to go back. We're leaving right now."

"*You there!*"

The voice belonged to a thin young man in dark slacks and white open-collared shirt who had entered the living room by way of a door to the basement. He approached the group warily.

"How did you—?" Then he saw the woman. He bowed. "Your Royal Highness."

"Anselm, show these people out. You know what to do."

"Of course, ma'am." Anselm showed a trace of a smile.

"I sort of figured that," Gene said, drawing his sword. Then his face fell, as if he suddenly realized something.

"Your sword will avail you nothing," Her Royal Highness said. "You are in the grip of forces beyond your understanding. Cooperate, or it will go badly for you."

"If you think I'm worried about this little pinhead," Gene said, jabbing toward Anselm, "think again."

Anselm's hand was a blur. It seemed to grow a wicked-looking automatic pistol. He pointed it at Gene. "You're the one who should go back to square one, friend." He grinned wickedly.

"You do have a point, Anselm old bean," Gene said, sheathing his sword.

"Very good, Anselm," the woman said. "How goes it?"

"All quiet, ma'am."

"Splendid. No sign of my brother?"

"None at all. May I ask how your battle fares?"

"Certainly. Deems and his men are holding their own in the outer quarters. Which is to say they are being slaughtered. But my spells sustain them. Even an armless corpse can be animated enough to block a demon's path. In the unlikely event my brother should discover the location of this portal, you will do your best to take him alive. Is that understood?"

"It will be done, ma'am."

"Good. I will put up the veil again."

The woman waved her hand and the portal became a dark oblong.

Anselm gestured with the gun. "Okay, down those stairs, all of you. But first get rid of all that steel. Throw them in a pile . . . there."

Snowy, Gene, and Kwip tossed their swords and daggers on the floor near a red leather easy chair.

"Right. Now, down the steps, single file. And I'll shoot the first one who thinks about . . ."

Outside, the night erupted in fireworks.

Gene yelled, "Rush 'em, Snowy!"

But Snowy had already begun his leap. Anselm squawked, stepped back, and fired. Snowy hit him first, then Gene jumped on top. The three of them rolled around the carpet until Kwip jumped on the pile. The tangle of arms and legs became a beast that shambled about the living room, upsetting end tables here and there.

"Jesus Christ!" Gene yelled finally, springing to his feet. Everyone unpiled, got up, and stepped back warily.

Anselm rose to his feet. Something strange was happening to him. Parts of his skin had cracked like an ill-fitting rubber suit. The cracks revealed an interior yellow-orange glow. The fissures veined out and widened, and the skin fell away in swatches, revealing the demon body within. The demon swelled to full volume as it shed its outer camouflage. The last of the skin and clothing dropped off as the eerily glowing creature topped seven and a half feet.

"YOU WILL DIE, HUMAN SCUM! ALL OF YOU!"

The house lights went out.

ESTATE

"WHAT KIND OF deal did you have in mind?" Incarnadine asked the enormous apparition that had appeared above the house.

"I'm sure we can work something out, Inky old friend."

"I don't share your optimism. What do you have to offer, aside from what already belongs to me?"

"Well, we're not exactly offering anything, my dear Inky. In fact—"

"*I am not your 'dear Inky'!* I am Incarnadine, Liege Lord, Imperator and Gatekeeper of the Western Pale, and, by the grace of the gods, *King* and Sovereign Ruler of Ylium, Zephorea, Halmudia, Grekoran, and West Thurlangia! You have our leave to address us as 'Your Serene and Transcendent Majesty.'"

The face raised its eyebrows. "Touchy, aren't we? As I was saying . . . *Your Majesty* . . . you're not exactly in the best bargaining position imaginable. Now are you?"

"Why not?"

"We have the castle. In a very short time we will cut off the only access you have to it."

"Which means that you haven't overrun Ferne's position yet."

"A formality. What are mortals against us? Chopped liver, that's what."

"Well, what's taking you so long?"

"I have to admit your sister's not chopped liver. And neither are you, Ink—er, Your Majesty. Neither are you. Really, I mean it! Look, let's be frank. All cards faceup. I mean, *obviously* we have a stalemate here. I think it's high time we all sat down and had a serious talk about what we're going to do about the situation. Share ideas. Exchange information. Get to know each other."

Incarnadine nodded. "Sounds very cozy. I will also be frank. I'd sooner bed down with scorpions than sit at a bargaining table with the likes of you."

The face looked hurt. "Really, that's not very nice."

"You know that the moment I get back inside the castle, your game is through."

"I don't know that at all. You might not be aware of this, but the barrier your great-great-great-great—"

"You've actually kept track?"

"—great-great-great grandfather erected to keep us out of the castle is *gone*, Your Super-Terrific Majesty. Zip-bang, not there anymore. Okay? So, don't go making threats you can't follow through with."

Incarnadine was silent a moment, then said, "I really must compliment you on having mastered the local vernacular so quickly."

The face couldn't help being pleased. "That? It's nothing. This is one world we're going to insist on keeping. We work right into the mythology so well, it's as though it had been created with us in mind."

"If you look back far enough into your historical records, you might find that you did have a hand in working up the indigenous mythology, or at least inspiring it."

"Really? That's very interesting. But back to business. Isn't it clear that you will have to share power at some point? You people can't keep us back forever."

"I don't see why not," Incarnadine said. "In any event, I certainly won't be the one to give away the family business."

"Oh, you wouldn't be giving away all of it, now would you?"

"You would never be content with partial control, were I willing to grant it."

"Come now. I think it's about time you realized that your attitude toward us is really the result of years of propaganda. We get the worst press imaginable. Your family always had it in for us. It's not fair! We've done nothing, absolutely nothing to justify being treated so shabbily all these years. Discrimination! That's what it is, pure and simple."

"You have my sympathies. My advice to you is this—pull back your forces now. If you fail to do so, you will be destroyed."

The head shook sadly. "Really, Inky. I thought better of you."

Incarnadine raised both hands and began to trace a pattern in the air. *"Foul spirit, destroyer of worlds, blasphemer and ancient enemy! I bid you begone, in the name of all the gods of all the universes—get thee hence! Flee the wrath of the righteous, and trouble the innocent no more! Depart, I say!"*

The face contorted with pain. The mouth opened, and a wailing cry pierced the night.

"Bastard human!" it screamed. "Filthy pile of excrement! You had your chance! Now you'll suffer everlasting torment! You'll all suffer horribly and die! You, your family, and all the get of the Haplodie! Die, you'll all die, die, die—"

Abruptly the apparition disappeared.

Trent said, "They really do fear you."

"Of course," Incarnadine said as he finished up the spell. "Their only hope was to take me out—here, in this world, where I was handicapped."

"Will it be necessary to push the castle through another magical transformation in order to get rid of them?"

"No, not with all the modifications I made when I recast the transmogrification spell. I can now draw all the power I want without the risk of blowing the spell by overloading it. Which was always a limitation, as you know. I installed a circuit breaker, so to speak."

"Nice touch," Trent said. "But we have to get you back inside the castle before you can tap any of that power."

"Not necessarily. Not if what I've been working on for the last few days proves fruitful."

"What's that? I thought you were trying to summon the portal."

"I gave up on that fairly quick. It was obvious someone had it nailed down. No, I came up with a gimmick that might allow me to tap castle power by means of an inductance effect through interuniversal space. I say might, because it hasn't worked so far. But now the portal is close at hand, and that might make a difference. I'm going to try it, anyway. I'll disconnect from your system first. Cover me."

"Go ahead," Trent said. "And good luck."

As Incarnadine made movements with his hands, things sprang into existence in the hayfield and in the general vicinity of the manor house. Swirling pillars of fire blazed up. Hordes of sword-wielding monsters charged. Various airborne improbabilities commenced their unlikely maneuvers. The sky opened up and began to rain fire and brimstone, and fingers of lightning jabbed at the earth.

"They're really slinging the crap now," Trent said edgily. "Everything they have, it looks like. This isn't going to be easy, Inky, castle power or no."

"Piece of cake, Trent old fellow," the King of West Thurlangia said as multicolored pyrotechnics spewed from his fingertips.

Hand in hand with Deena, Barnaby stumbled up the stairs. Darkness above. He reached a landing, turned, and kept climbing. He didn't like this option, but the demon had come from the basement, and he didn't relish going down there. He and Deena had to hide out somewhere, and the ground floor was out, having erupted into a melee soon after the lights had gone out.

They reached the top of the stairs and a long hallway, along which a few doors were set. Barnaby tried the first and found it locked, as was the second, but the third, which lay at the end of an L, opened onto a dark, sparsely furnished bedroom. They went in and closed the door.

"I'm hidin' in here," Deena said, sliding back the closet door. It was a walk-in closet, quite spacious enough to be considered a small room. Barnaby rolled the door shut, and they stood in darkness with their arms around each other.

"I don't know if I like this," Deena said.

Horrible noises came from the first floor: shouts, exclamations, the sounds of furniture smashing, and the odd demoniacal howl.

Barnaby eased the closet door open and looked out. The rectangle of the bedroom window flashed incessantly as the battle raged outside.

"Still shootin' out there?" Deena whispered.

"I don't think it's shooting, exactly," Barnaby said. "I don't really know what the hell it is. We couldn't be on Earth, because nothing like this goes on there."

"How do you know?"

Another voice in the closet said, "Can't you people see I'm busy in here? Damn inconsiderate!"

Deena tried to climb Barnaby like a ladder. Barnaby toppled backward into a tangle of clothes and coat hangers.

A match was lit and put to a candle. The form of a squatting demon became visible in the far end of the closet. Beneath its haunches the carpet had been rolled back, and a pentagram, executed in precise chalk lines, was inscribed on the oak flooring underneath.

It was a different sort of demon from the one they had seen before. Smaller, and having a somewhat rounder head, its coloring was a ghastly, cadaverous gray. Purple wormlike growths festooned the right side of its face, and festering sores afflicted its hide at various locations.

Its humanlike face registered extreme pique. "You think this is easy with all these distractions?" it demanded to know. "*You* try to cast an effective spell with all this commotion going on. And then if something screws up, it's *your* ass is on the grill. Try working under those conditions! And you just come waltzing in here without so much as knocking! Unbelievable!"

"Sorry!" Barnaby said after spitting out one end of a feather boa. He tried to get to his feet.

"Barnaby!" Deena screamed, pounding on his back. "Let's get outta here!"

"Capital idea!" the demon agreed.

It took some doing. The sliding door was stuck, caught on some debris. Finally Barnaby succeeded in rolling it back, and he and Deena crashed through into the bedroom along with a shower of hangers, peignoirs, shoe boxes, and other paraphernalia.

"I'm complaining to my union about this," came a muttering from the closet. "Just you wait and see!"

Downstairs, Sheila huddled behind a sofa, calmly shifting lines of force with the power of her will. There were lines that ran crosswise—north-south (magnetic fields?)—and lines that ran perpendicular, east-west, and she had no idea what those were. All she knew, in this early stage of her understanding of Earth's magical forces, was that allocating power was a matter of shifting those lines around. Of course, what she really didn't understand was the power source that seemed very near. She couldn't fathom why there would be such a strong one so close by. She knew now that certain points of the Earth's surface, certain features of the landscape, contained great power, and she sensed quite a few of those out there, somewhere, but this nearby power source was different. Anyway, she was tapping it, too. Probably badly, very inefficiently, but she was getting power from it.

She seemed to be able to see what was happening in the living room, even though she had her eyes closed. Snowy and Gene were each battling a demon, the second demon having appeared shortly after the first one had revealed itself. Snowy and Gene were doing fairly well. They would be dead in an instant if Sheila were to stop helping them, feeding them the magical energy that transformed them into superhuman (in Gene's case; super-whatever in Snowy's) swordfighters.

Whoops! Another demon. Better do a Linda and split off . . . Snowy. Yeah, split off Snowy into twins. Wait. Was that demon another demon, or a doppelganger? If it was, it was a good one, so no matter.

By the way, where was Linda? Still hiding behind the settee; good. She was out of this, no magic at all. What about the others? The one with the beard was fighting. The small guy, the librarian, was—in the library! That guy really liked books! But there were others. A guy and a black girl? Sheila couldn't get a fix on them.

A fourth demon? Good Lord. Well, now she'd have to split Gene off, too.

They approached the house, firing continuously at unnamed and unnameable things which attacked from every quarter. A trouble-some phenomenon was developing off to the left: thin, glowing tentacles like animated garden hoses snaking through the grass, trying for encirclement. Incarnadine tried bearing to the right, but two filaments met in front of him and completed the circle. Sheets of flame rose to form a dome of fire around the brothers. Incarnadine halted. He shouted a six-syllable word twice, the first time in a normal pitch, the second in falsetto. The dome broke apart, boiling away into pink smoke.

"Nice work!" Trent called. "Hey, I think it's going to be all ri—"

Trent leaped over the rapidly widening crack in the earth that had opened at his feet. Smoke and fire issued from deep within the chasm. The crack branched off and clove the earth near Incarna-dine, who leaped to the right, then did a hop, skip, and jump over a series of smaller lateral fissures that gaped in front of him.

Then the earth settled down, and the brothers continued their advance.

Streamers of scintillation had begun forming in the air around the house. They did not look particularly dangerous to Incarnadine, and he decided they were probably by-products rather than defensive phenomena, but he kept glancing at them occasionally as he walked and fired, mindful that they could develop into something.

As he swung his sword again and again, Gene wondered why his castle-bred skills were still with him, here, on Earth. He was thankful that they were. He would have been reduced to cold cuts otherwise.

Gene parried a wicked crosswise cut, sparks shooting off his blade. He riposted with a lunge, then feinted to the demon's right side. He whirled, did a backflip, landed on his haunches, and slashed at the demon's legs, cutting them neatly in two at the knee joints. The body toppled over an upturned chair.

Gene lurched to his feet in time to beat off a lunge by another demon. He backtracked, steadied his footing, then parried three quick cuts, riposting to his opponent's head. He feinted to the thorax, then quickly jabbed at the eyes again. The demon backed off.

Snowy's sword was like the blade of a whirling fan. He was up against two opponents and holding his own.

He was thinking of how hungry he was.

"Somethin's happening out there!" Deena said, peeking out the dormer window.

They had found a relatively demon-free spare bedroom. Barnaby rose and looked out the window. It was hard to describe what was going on. There were two arenas of special interest: one, what was happening out in the field in back of the house; two, what was gathering around the house itself. The latter involved sparkling auroral displays that fluttered like sheets hung out to dry in a high wind. As he and Deena watched, the phenomenon grew more intense, partially blocking their view of the strange battle that raged in the backyard.

Barnaby sank to the bed. "I can't watch anymore. Is the door locked?"

"Yeah. No, let me check it."

Deena returned. "Yeah, it's locked. I—what the *hell* are you doin'?"

"I'm tired," Barnaby said as he turned down the bedding. "I'm going to try to get some shut-eye."

"You gonna what? You're crazy!"

Barnaby crawled between the covers. "What else is there to do? We can't get out of here. We might as well die in bed as anywhere else. Besides, if I'm dreaming all this, maybe I'll wake up."

"Well, move over."

Deena climbed in with him. They looked at each other, then pulled the covers over their heads.

"Singularity vortex!" Trent yelled over the noise of battle.

"Yeah!" Incarnadine agreed. That was what the sparkling streamers that had enveloped the house were beginning ominously to look like. The flux of magical energies in and around the house and its environs were starting to warp the fabric of normal spacetime. If the process continued, the house would drop right out of the continuum, possibly taking the portal along with it. Incarnadine wasn't sure exactly what would happen to the portal, but it would be nothing good; of that he was certain.

"We have to get in there," Incarnadine shouted, unsure of being heard. A six-legged, three-horned quasi-rhinoceros charged at him. He sprayed it with green fire; the thing fissioned into six smaller animals. He laid down a blanket of fire over these. Result: three dozen reduced-scale replicas, all maniacally bent on goring him in the ankles. They continued to replicate and reduce in size, Zeno's paradox coming into play. They would keep halving the distance to their target, but never reach it. Incarnadine stepped out of their path.

There was less and less to do. Another antique aircraft circled overhead, but was not quite so magically well constituted as its predecessors; its motor sputtered, then died, and the craft fell out of the night, crashing into the formal garden on the house's east side.

More monsters, these looking a bit threadbare: another reject from a Japanese sci fi flick; a dozen more hackneyed horrors from central casting; something that looked from the waist up like Lon Chaney's werewolf, but was web-toed and scaly in the other direction. It blew up very nicely. A second anomaly shambled toward them, looking for all the world like a gorilla wearing a vintage deep-sea diving helmet. Whatever movie it was from, it didn't get very far.

There came a lull in the action.

With a weary sigh, Trent sank to one knee. "Man, I'm bushed." He chuckled. "Getting old."

"I think we've just about broken their back."

Trent surveyed the field of battle, now empty. "No, they have something left."

"I'd be willing to bet not. That last salvo had spell exhaustion written all over it."

"Maybe so. We'd best make a run for the house now before that vortex—" Trent reconsidered. "Hell, maybe we don't want to get to the house. I'm not sure I can deal with any continuum disturbances."

"I'm fairly sure I can," Incarnadine said. "Let's move."

Trent got up. "Whatever you say. You seem to be running the show now."

"I still need your help. Got your second wind?"

"I'm on my fifth, I think. I've lost count. You know, that inductance gimmick really—"

The earth began to shake, and thunder rolled across the meadow.

"Oh, hell," Trent said. "Here comes the finale."

The thunder reached a crescendo, then a brilliant flash lit up the countryside.

All Hell came at them. Incarnadine looked out across the meadow and saw the Hosts of Hell in full battle regalia, arrayed to meet the foe. There were fiends, demons, hobgoblins, imps, and incubi of every description. Some sat astride great horned beasts of battle, some rode fantastic metal engines. Most charged on foot, screaming bloody mayhem.

Incarnadine flamed the first wave. They went down easily enough, but there were simply too many of them. He prepared himself for death, reciting the first lines of the Prayer of Leave-taking.

He looked up and saw a burnished curving blade poised to strike. The scaled horror that wielded it regarded him with molten red eyes.

"Now you will die, Haplodite scum," the thing said to him.

"You send me to a better place, tiresome one," the King replied.

"You—you. . . .!" The thing was beside itself with rage. But it did not strike.

"What seems to be the matter, O Fearful One?"

"You . . . *shit!*"

Incarnadine laughed. He laid his palms on the thing's horny chest and pushed. There was almost nothing to push against. The matinee monster fell over like a papier-mâché dummy.

He materialized a sword and swung at another bugaboo. It split down the middle, revealing its chintzy hollowness.

"Spell exhaustion!" he heard Trent yell. "Inky! They've shot their wad! They're just buying time."

"The house is about to go!" he shouted back. "Let's get up there!"

It was easier said than done. They were flapped, batted, and swatted at by hosts of bogus fiends, all about as substantial as paper dolls, and as dangerous. But there were thousands of them, and they succeeded in getting in the way.

Trent and Incarnadine hedge-hopped through the formal gardens, then encountered more ersatz boogeymen on the croquet court. They pushed, kicked, and bulled their way forward, finally reaching the outer perimeter of the auroralike phenomenon. Once inside it, the cheapjack monsters disappeared.

Invisible fists pummeled them, jostling them this way and that. Fierce gusts of wind arose and tore at them. Leaning into the wind, they staggered forward. After fighting their way across a brick patio, they reached the back door.

Incarnadine began waving his hands. Trent tried the handle. The door opened. Trent grinned at his brother.

"You probably still can't spell 'magician.'"

"I was always an overachiever."

At that moment, the bottom dropped out of everything.

HOUSE OVER THE BORDERLINE

"BARNABY?"

"Huh?"

"Wake up."

"I'm up. Whaddya want?"

"What do I want? We were kissin', and then you go and fall asleep on me!"

"I didn't fall asleep."

"Yes, you did!"

"I'm sorry. I feel like I haven't slept in a thousand years."

"Yeah, me, too. But I was beginning to like what we were doin'. A whole lot."

"You mean this stuff?"

After they parted, she said, "Yeah, that stuff. And a couple of other things you were startin' to do."

A strange flickering light suddenly dawned through the window.

"Uh-oh," Deena said.

"That was quick. Sun just popped up, I guess."

"The sun don't pop up, never."

"Look out the window."

"You look out the window!"

"I'm tired, Deena honey."

"And I ain't? Oh, damn it, all right."

Deena got to her knees and leaned out over the nightstand and peeked out the window. Then she dove back into bed.

"What was out there?" he asked.

"Don't ask!" she said.

The bedroom door burst open and the demon they had encountered in the closet came scampering in. It went directly to the window and threw up the sash.

"Excuse me, folks, but it's time to bail out," the fiend said as it clambered up onto the sill. "So long!" It jumped off and was gone.

"Don't that beat everything," Deena said.

"You know, he wasn't such a bad sort, once you got to know him."

"Kiss me again, fool."

The demons were dead. Very dead. In fact, they stank badly enough to have succumbed days ago, and looked it as well.

"This one just crumpled up and died, all of a sudden like," Snowclaw said (in his own language, but everyone seemed to understand him).

"Mine, too," Gene said. "Jesus. There were only two of them."

"There may be others," Kwip said.

"Nope," Sheila said. "Those are the two who were causing all the trouble. The rest was magic."

"What in the world is going on outside?" Linda asked.

They all went to the window.

"Now this is extremely interesting," Gene said.

Outside, the sun was a golden arch across the sky, the moon a pale silver bow. The landscape was alive. Saplings grew into giant trees, died, decayed, and fell in a matter of seconds. The seasons went by, one after another, in a flickering blur.

"We're traveling through time," Gene decided. "I guess."

"That's absolutely correct," came a voice from the far end of the living room.

Gene and his companions turned to regard the two men who had entered the room.

"Hello again," said the tall, handsome man with the beard.

"Lord Incarnadine!" Linda said.

"Yes. You remembered. I believe we met only once."

"Certainly I remember . . . uh, Your Majesty." Linda did a quick curtsey.

"And I believe this is . . . Mr. Ferraro?"

"Yes, sir."

"And . . . ?"

"Kwip of Dunwiddin, Your Majesty."

"No need to kneel. Arise, Kwip of Dunwiddin!"

"His Majesty is too kind."

"And, let me see . . ."

"They call me Snowclaw."

"Aptly yclept. Stout fellow. And this charming young lady?"

"Sheila Jankowski, sir."

"Ah, it was you. You were doing quite a good deal of spellcasting in here, weren't you?"

Sheila blushed. "Yes, sir."

"Excellent work! You saved the lives of your friends, and quite possibly mine and my brother's. I'm sorry—ladies and gentlemen, may I present His Royal Highness Trent, Prince of the House of Haplodie, Protector of Zilonesia, Vice-regent of Ulontha, Beloved of the Gods, Holy Warrior, Keeper of the Stone of Truth-telling . . . and so forth and so on."

Trent said, "Those honorifics and fifty cents will get me a cup of decaffeinated coffee. Howdy, folks."

Gene said, "Uh . . . sir? May I ask a question?"

"Sure," Incarnadine said.

"What the hell has been going on?"

Incarnadine laughed. "That's going to take some explaining."

Linda said, "I want to know where *those* things came from." She pointed to the cadavers.

"From a very mysterious aspect, the nature of which we might never fully understand."

"Are they *real* demons? I mean—well, it's kind of hard to ask the right questions."

"I know what you mean. Are they truly supernatural? I don't know. I suspect the physical laws that govern their universe are radically different from most. They do have physical bodies, however, so, as I see it, the question is moot. I'm sorry I don't have many of the right answers."

"That's okay."

Incarnadine went to the window. "Don't let all this nonsense out the window faze you. Too much magic in one place tends to be a little destabilizing. Not to worry. We thought the trajectory might turn out to be hyperbolic, but it isn't. The effect will start to rebound momentarily. There we go."

As he spoke, the sun stopped in the sky over what looked like a Carboniferous swamp. Then it began to move backward. Night fell, giving way to dawn a few seconds later. The sun streaked back across the sky, accelerating at a rapid rate. Soon the golden arch re-established itself.

"I'm getting a Big Mac attack," Gene said.

"As I said," Incarnadine continued, "not to worry. The house should return to normal spacetime in short order. Any other questions?"

"This is Earth, isn't it?" Sheila asked. "I mean, when we get back to normal . . . whatever it was you said."

"Yes, this is Earth. Your home. And no doubt you want to stay."

"Yes! I mean . . ."

"There is some doubt?"

"Well, I'm going to miss the castle." Sheila slapped her forehead. "I don't believe I said that." Then she realized the gaffe. "I didn't mean—"

Incarnadine chuckled. "I know exactly what you mean. And I've been meaning to solve the one-way access problem for a long time. Please accept my apologies for any inconvenience the delay has caused you. Now that we have the Earth portal nailed down, I think we should establish a permanent access to the castle. This house would make an excellent way station."

"Where is this place?" Gene asked.

Trent said, "The closest town is Ligonier, Pennsylvania."

Gene jumped up and down. "That's a stone's throw from my hometown!"

"Mine, too!" Sheila said.

Gene stopped jumping. "How the hell am I going to explain where I've been? I've been away almost a year."

Incarnadine thought about it. "Well, this is a problem. There are some possible solutions, though. As you can see, we're traveling through time. It could be possible to stop the house just shortly after the time you entered the castle. We could cut it as close as you like. Or, as an alternative, it's actually theoretically possible to tune a portal to permit time travel. You have to be careful to avoid paradoxes, of course. Meeting yourself coming the other way, that sort of thing. But in principle, it shouldn't be a problem.''

"I'll opt for the portal method," Gene said. "I'd like time to change into something less Gothic."

"No doubt."

"Sir, what about the situation back at the castle?"

"Well, as soon as we get things squared away here, I'm going to return to the castle to finish some important business."

"My liege!"

Carrying a large leather-bound book, his index finger wedged inside it, Osmirik ran into the room and knelt at his liege lord's feet.

"Arise, good and faithful servant. Whaddya got there?"

"The spell, Your Majesty! The containment spell for the Hosts of Hell! Your ancestor, Ervoldt, used this ancient Tryphosite spell for confining evil spirits. I've done a rough translation of some of the more obscure lines." He fumbled with a few sheets of paper.

Incarnadine scanned the book. "Tryphosite, eh? You don't say. Ervoldt was a wise old coot, wasn't he? Yes, yes, I see. This should work. Excellent job, Osmirik. I knew I could count on you."

"I am only too happy to be of service to His Serene and Transcendent Majesty."

"This looks like it has a decay time of a little over five thousand years. No wonder Ferne unraveled it so easily. It was just about due to go on the fritz, anyway. Do you suppose if we made some modifications we could increase the effective time—say, here . . . and here?"

Osmirik looked over the King's shoulder. "Oh, I should say so, Your Majesty."

Incarnadine read the section through again, nodding. "Yes, it should work." He closed the book and handed it back to the librarian. "Thank you, Osmirik. I am forever in your debt."

Astonished, Osmirik accepted the volume. "His Majesty does not need a working copy . . . ?"

Incarnadine smiled. "You needn't bother. I'm a fast study."

Awed, Osmirik bowed and backed away.

Incarnadine looked out the window. "The house will probably oscillate a little before it settles down to the present. A half hour, I'd say. Did anyone check out the kitchen? There might be something to eat in there. Is anyone as famished as I am?"

* * *

The house bounced for two full hours between the future and the past until eventually zeroing in on its target, the fleeting instant of the present. In the meantime, they ate a meal of canned food made tolerable by an excellent Chablis that Gene found in the cellar, along with many other drinkable spirits. Barnaby and Deena came down in time for dessert: canned cherries jubilee with a superb Napoleon brandy.

"There was more demons upstairs," Deena told them. "We saw one of them!"

"An incubus," Incarnadine said. "A technician, probably. Blue-collar type, not one of the warrior demons of the sort you people battled. Relatively harmless."

"Do you think any of them are still here?" Barnaby wanted to know.

"No," Trent said. "If the warriors died of spell exhaustion, the underlings didn't have a chance."

Deena told of the one who had jumped out the window.

"One chance in a million of survival that way. Not that it's any great loss."

They all agreed not to lose any sleep over it.

"How did they manage to fool your sister?" Gene asked.

"Well, their disguises fooled you," Incarnadine said. "Didn't they? But you're right, my sister should have known better. I suspect she succumbed to their influence a long time ago."

"You mean, she was a puppet?"

"No. The Hosts are persuasive. I've told you how, as young people, we all had a brief flirtation with them. She was acting in their interests all along, and I don't think she realized it. Of course, this in no way exonerates her."

Sheila said, "When you go back to the castle, you don't expect to have any trouble?"

"None," Incarnadine said, finishing the last of his wine. "I can beat them, and they know it now. Their only chance was to kill me, or keep me out of the castle. They couldn't do the former and they can't do the latter."

"Couldn't they—?" Sheila shook her head, puzzled.

"No, they're licked. Sure, they could battle me every inch of the way back to their portal. But they know they'd lose in the end. I suspect they've totally withdrawn from the castle."

Sheila frowned. "It's so hard to understand."

"Yes, almost impossible. I don't pretend to understand them,

nor do I fully understand everything that's happened. But if Ferne
still alive, I'm hoping to get some answers." Incarnadine sat back.
"When I've finished in the castle, I'll send back word here, so you
can come on through, if you wish."

"I'm leaving from here," Sheila said. "I've only been gone a
few days."

"Fine. I'm sure you'll find a car in the garage. You're welcome
to use it."

"I still think I should do a time trip," Gene said. "And so
should Linda. Our folks will think we've come back from the
dead."

"Well, it will take some time to set up," Incarnadine said.

Trent said, "There's no need for that, if you want to take another
tack."

"How so?" Incarnadine asked.

Trent spoke to Gene. "Write a letter to your folks and make up
some good excuse for your absence. It's no problem for me to take
that letter and back-time it a year or so."

Incarnadine was surprised. "You've been dabbling in time
travel?"

"Sending people back is a little beyond my skill. But dropping a
few letters into the postal stream of twelve months ago would be a
breeze."

"Trent, I think you've become the family's best magician."

"Coming from you, that's quite a compliment."

"I like the idea," Gene said. "It means we could just pile into
the car with Sheila and drive home now. Those stories are going to
have to be pretty good, though. Now, let's see. What wild yarn
could we come up with?"

"Could somebody lend me plane fare to California?" Linda
asked.

"No problem," Trent said. "Put it on my MasterCard."

"Thanks. You're very kind."

"We princes are naturally charming."

"He's been using lines like that for three hundred years,"
Incarnadine warned.

"Go to hell, Inky."

Incarnadine rose from the table. "I think it's just about time."

CASTLE

THE TWO BROTHERS stepped through the veil their sister had erected to block the portal. Being of the House of Haplodie, they were immune; no spell could keep them out of the castle.

They found their sister Ferne slumped in a chair in the parlor, three empty sherry bottles at her feet. She was polishing off the remains of a fourth. Seeing Trent, dim recognition formed in her eyes.

" 'Lo," was all she managed, along with a twisted smile.

"Stay with her," Incarnadine said.

"For as long as I can," Trent said.

"What do you mean?"

"I can't stay in the castle for any length of time. It's the spell Dad laid on me when we had our difference of opinion. He banished me, Inky. Never told anyone. I guess he felt a little guilty."

Nonplussed, Incarnadine said, "What sort of spell?"

"Nothing much. It's just that if I stay here longer than, say, ten minutes, I begin to get a case of the paranoid heebie-jeebies. I just go quietly nuts and get this overwhelming urge to run screaming from the place. Very effective."

"Gods. I'm sorry, Trent. I wish I had known."

"Yeah. Well, I didn't tell anyone, for the shame of it all. Silly, I guess. It's not my fault Dad had it in for me."

Incarnadine felt restrained from commenting. "Uh, well, if you have to go—listen. Thanks. I'll never forget it, Trent."

"Don't mention it. Look me up next time you're in New York."

"I will."

They looked at each other for a long moment.

"Farewell, brother."

"Farewell," Incarnadine said. He turned and left the parlor.

He found Deems in the outer halls, along with the bodies of thousands of his men. Many had died of wounds, but more had succumbed to spell exhaustion. Judging from the number of enemy dead, they had given a good account of themselves, defending a strange castle in a foreign land.

Incarnadine took his overcoat off and covered his brother's body with it, then recited a prayer for the departed.

He walked a good distance into the castle before encountering carcasses of the previous invaders. The place already stank to high heaven. It would be a monumental cleanup job.

A whispering silence held throughout the castle. Death skulked in the shadows, but would not show its face. Time hung like cobwebs in the corners.

Incarnadine walked with purposeful stride. As he did, he got the feeling that someone or something was ahead of him, keeping just out of sight. He didn't see anything.

He knew exactly where to go. It was a long trip, and a lonely one. The years echoed in the halls, reverberating off stone-vaulted ceilings.

In a dim crypt in the nethermost reaches of the castle, he found what he sought. A black oblong lay inscribed in gray shadows. He approached it.

He heard his name called, far off, faint.

"No," he said.

Dim shapes swam within the portal, and a cold wind blew out of it. There came to his ears a faint wailing and weeping.

He ignored it, raising his hands. He began the spellcasting, reciting each line of the incantation crisply and distinctly. As he continued, the wailing grew louder and louder.

The spell was short, succinct, and to the point. He finished it with a flourish of his hands, and the sounds emanating from the portal ceased. He stepped forward and peered into the darkness. What had been a gaping hole was now a blank stone wall. He reached out and touched it. The portal was gone.

On his way back, he undid the protective spells over a few of the aspects his Guardsmen had retreated into along with most of the castle's local citizenry, and many of its Guests.

Tyrene, the captain of the Guard, was standing watch inside one of them. When the portal opened, Tyrene regarded his liege lord with some disgruntlement. Obviously he did not care for hiding out while the castle was overrun by invaders. But he had had his orders. Incarnadine did his best to assuage him and salve his wounded pride. Then he bade him sound recall.

Whistling a tune he had heard during his stay on Earth, he trudged up to his study to begin the job of bringing the castle back to life.